To J[...]

Your [...]

meant a lot to me.

My childhood dream was to
be a writer. At long last I am
fulfilling my dream.
I will always be
grateful for your encouragement.

Georgia
Zaslove

LifeRich Publishing is a registered trademark of The Reader's Digest Association, Inc.

LifeRich Publishing books may be ordered through booksellers or by contacting:

LifeRich Publishing
1663 Liberty Drive
Bloomington, IN 47403
www.liferichpublishing.com
1 (888) 238-8637

ISBN: 978-1-4897-2665-0 (sc)
ISBN: 978-1-4897-2666-7 (hc)
ISBN: 978-1-4897-2667-4 (e)

Library of Congress Control Number: 2020907250

Print information available on the last page.

LifeRich Publishing rev. date: 05/05/2020

This book is dedicated to Sy (Seymour) Rosenberg, James Lockard and Wayne Emmons, three brilliant attorneys from Memphis, Tennessee, who helped me write the trial in this book.

floor. He snarled, "What are you doing? Keep your hands off me!" Hope looked up at him in shock as he stepped over her. "Don't ever do that again. You're lucky I didn't knock you across the room, you stupid bitch."

For a moment, Hope sat on the floor—stunned, as though someone held her by the throat while she dangled, kicking desperately, trying to feel the ground beneath her feet. She tried to speak but could not. She wanted to get up, but her body rejected her desire to be in control. Instead, she rolled into a ball and covered her face with her hands, shaking as she cried in silence. Sammy hated it when she cried aloud.

She heard Sammy go into the hall bathroom. When he came out, he acted as if nothing had happened and hollered, "Let's eat!"

Hope pulled herself together, thinking that after he ate and calmed down she could try to get him to talk to her about what was so upsetting. They sat down to eat without one word from Sammy. Hope stared at her plate and pushed her mashed potatoes into piles while intermittently taking small bites. The ordeal had destroyed her appetite, and the smell was making her nauseated. She picked up the bottle of wine near her and poured a glass for herself and Sammy. She filled his glass to the brim and carefully pushed it to him.

He smiled and said, "Thank you, sweetheart." That was his sign that he was sorry. That was all Hope needed to feel better. She waited until he finished his wine, and she poured him a second glass before trying to have a conversation with him.

"Honey, you know Diane and Michael's two-year wedding anniversary is coming up, and I made reservations at Paulette's to take them out for dinner on Saturday night. I made the reservation for seven. Is that time okay with you?"

"That's fine."

"We also have the Katz's bar mitzvah on Saturday morning. Will you be able to go with me?"

He frowned as he gulped his wine. "I'll try, but don't count on me. I'll be working on the brownstone project. I plan to be there all day. I need to go over all the expenditures with Alfred. We're way over budget, and I can't seem to make him understand we have to watch every dime and get the first phase finished and sold so we can finance the second phase."

"Is that what you are so upset about today?"

"That and all the other crap I have to deal with. You have no idea the kind of jerks I deal with every day—customers badgering me for more of a discount, always wanting more for less. You would think I was running a business for charity. You wouldn't understand, because you've never had to deal with stress on a daily basis. And don't tell me playing the piano for the symphony once in a while is your big contribution. I'm the one who pays for everything around here."

"Honey, I know you work hard and have always taken good care of me. I just wanted to help if I could. I don't know what I can do if you don't tell me. There must be something I can do."

He hissed. "There is—stop hovering over me and asking what's wrong. I can handle my problems myself. I don't need your nagging."

Hope recoiled and went silent, knowing one wrong word could incite another brutal response.

The next morning, Hope got out of bed and contemplated calling her sister, Rachel. She wanted to talk to her about Sammy's latest temper tantrum that, for Hope, had ended in confusion and frustration. What was he hiding? For the life of her, she could not understand how to get him to open up and just say what he was thinking.

She waited until she heard Sammy leave before going to the kitchen to make her coffee. Knowing it was too early to call her sister, she poured a steaming cup of coffee and decided to write her thoughts down in a letter to her husband. She considered that maybe he would not be so defensive when he read it and would think it through before responding. She ascended the entry hall stairs on her way to her room and gazed at the photos artistically arranged on the wall. It was the story of their life together. It started with their wedding picture, followed by milestones from their twenty-eight years of marriage. Her mood began to sink as she looked over them. *What have I done so wrong?* As she entered her bedroom, she stopped to admire their magnificent four-poster canopy bed with gorgeous gold-and-red silk brocade cascading into a puddle on the Persian rug. She thought about all the things that she had done to

3

make a romantic bedroom for them: choosing rich colors and antique furniture, building a walk-in closet, and designing an elaborate master bath, all to please him. But for what? He seldom came into the room, let alone slept in it. She sat down at her antique secretary and began to write. The more she wrote, the more despondent she became. Tears filled her eyes and dropped onto the page, blurring the words. The phone's loud ring jolted her out of her melancholy. As she picked up, she heard a familiar voice that always made her feel better—Rachel's.

"Hey, sis. How are you doing?"

Hope, always stoic, took a deep breath before answering. "Fine. What are you doing up so early?"

Rachel laughed. "I couldn't sleep last night. No reason. Just one of those nights. So, I got up and went to work early. What are you up to today?"

"Not much. I'm going to the gym, trying to build my stamina back up."

She could hear herself talking, but all she could think about was the craziness with Sammy. She was grateful her sister had called. She needed someone to talk to—someone whom she could say anything to without being judged, chastised, or ridiculed. Even though Rachel had heard the same complaints many times, she would always be patient and kind. Hope had wrestled for years with the idea of getting a divorce. However, she had always justified her commitment to stay, reasoning that divorce was *not* something they did in their family. No one was divorced. Their motto was "Murder maybe, divorce never."

She spaced out while listening to Rachel talk about needing to deliver some documents to Syrus's law offices—things he had left at home in his rush to get to court. Then Hope heard her ask about the bar mitzvah on Saturday and whether they were going.

Hope responded, "I was planning on going, but I don't know about Sammy. He's tied up with the brownstone project, and it's making him crazy. Matter of fact, we had another hideous fight last night."

"Oh no. Well, don't feel bad. I doubt Syrus will make it to the bar mitzvah either. He's the defense attorney for the guy who raped and murdered the twelve-year-old child. Sy will probably be strategizing

4

with his team all weekend, so social events are the least of his concerns." Rachel's voice became a thorny growl. "Because he's got to protect the murderer from going to jail. Anyway, I called to see if you wanted to go to lunch. There's a new restaurant in the Cooper-Young district. They make their own bread and grow their own vegetables with no toxic chemicals. Everyone says it's great, and I've wanted to try it. Why don't I pick you up after I leave Sy's office?"

"Sounds great. Just honk when you get here. Bye."

Hope felt better as she slid the letter into a drawer and closed up the desk.

2

SYRUS "SY" MARCUS WALKED THROUGH THE COURTHOUSE WITH A determined gait, his head held high, his intense eyes taking in everyone and everything around him. He was quick to smile and reach his hand out in friendship to all he knew. Dressed in a perfectly tailored suit and polished shoes, he exuded the strength and precision of one who has served in the military. As Syrus neared the courtroom where his case was being heard, his law clerk rose to greet him.

Syrus whispered to his clerk as they headed into the courtroom, "It seems we may not have a verdict." Buoyantly, Sy charged to the defense table and sat next to his client, Buford Hollis. He leaned in to whisper, "I think we still have a hung jury. I don't think the judge will make them go back a third time to deliberate."

The court clerk announced, "Will the defendant please rise."

Syrus and Mr. Hollis were quick to stand at attention, both looking straight ahead with resolute expressions.

The judge turned to the jury. "Have you reached a verdict?"

The foreman of the jury stood and answered, "We have not, Your Honor; I'm sorry, but we're never going to agree."

The judge's shoulders drooped as he took a deep, labored breath;

shook his head; and announced, "Well, I have no choice but to declare a mistrial. I am going to continue the conditions of the bail order, pending the prosecution's decision for a new trial."

Buford Hollis, a short, scrawny man in his mid-thirties, oblivious to the outraged reaction of the courtroom spectators, lowered his head and stared at his worn but polished shoes.

The parents of the raped and murdered twelve-year-old girl began to wail as family and friends rushed to comfort them. The mother of the dead child screamed at the accused, but he did not acknowledge her pain, ignoring the anger being hurled at him.

The accused barely moved as he looked up at Syrus and, in an emotionless monotone, said, "You were worth every dime. Now can you help me get out the back way? I ain't going through that mess of reporters."

Sy motioned to his law clerk. "Take Mr. Hollis out the back way and then get back to the office. Tell Dottie I'll be back after lunch." Sy waited for the courtroom to empty before leaving.

A crowd of reporters and the public were gathered outside the courthouse waiting for the jury to leave. A TV reporter stopped the foreman of the jury as he tried to push his way through the crowd.

A cameraman stood behind the reporter, and another cameraman stood to the side, trying to get as many people in the shot as possible. Don Heller, a wiry, hawkish-looking man who worked for the *Memphis Daily News* stood behind the reporter, recording every word with his handheld tape recorder.

The TV reporter shoved a microphone in the foreman's face. "You were the foreman in this trial; was there anything the jury *could* agree on?"

The foreman, a rugged-looking man in an ill-fitting suit, replied, "Well, 'bout the only thing any of us could agree on was if *we* was ever in trouble, we'd want that Syrus Marcus for our lawyer."

Sy was walking in the opposite direction of the crowd, trying to get away unnoticed. However, someone did notice him and yelled, "There he is! That's the sorry bastard that got him off!" The crowd instantly moved in to confront Syrus as the TV reporter ran, thrusting his microphone forward, leading the crowd gallantly with his saber of choice.

The TV reporter jabbed the microphone into Sy's face. He jerked back. "Mr. Marcus, Mr. Marcus … it took the jury two days to come back with no decision. What do you think kept them from convicting this man?"

"I have no idea; I am not allowed to confer with the jury," Sy said.

"People are outraged when a murderer gets off in a case like this, where the evidence is overwhelming. How do you sleep at night?"

Sy kept his cool as he replied, "The evidence was circumstantial, so it becomes a matter of opinion—in this case, the jury's opinion. Obviously, they did not believe the evidence proved beyond a reasonable doubt that he was guilty."

"But—"

"Sorry, no more questions." Sy pushed his way out of the crowd and headed for his car. The crowd continued to hurl ugly accusations at him as he quickened his pace to get away.

He drove to his favorite hole-in-the-wall restaurant, Joe's Café, a place where he did not run into other lawyers. He didn't want to talk about the case or be bothered. A wonderful black family owned the restaurant. He had saved their teenage son from going to jail for loitering—a typical bullshit charge. Henceforth, they treated him like a king when there. As he entered the restaurant, he smiled and greeted the owner and then motioned to the bartender, ordering a Stoli on the rocks before being seated at the table of his choice. As always, everyone was happy to see him—a nice change after the assault he had just endured. However, underneath his calm facade, he was livid. He was tired of people blaming the lawyer when it was his job to defend his client. It was not his job to decide whether his client was innocent or guilty; that was the jury's job. Sy realized part of his anger came from his own belief Buford could have been guilty, but he had been hired to defend him either way. It wasn't his fault the evidence was iffy at best. The little girl had been raped anally, making it impossible to get reliable DNA. When she was discovered, her clothes were missing, and she had on only shoes and socks, which turned up no DNA evidence. No one had seen Buford at the scene, and he had a solid alibi. Even though his client had a past accusation of rape on record, it was not admissible in court. He had been accused, not convicted, so it did not make him guilty and there wasn't any proof that he was involved. A lot of innocent men were in jail for lesser reasons, and Sy never wanted to be responsible for letting an innocent man go to prison. These days however, more outrage was directed at the lawyers than the alleged criminals, and he was sick of it. To top it off, his wife was talking divorce—the last thing he wanted. In his mind, they had always had a good marriage. Yes, he worked long hours, and he was taking those damn pills for high blood pressure that interfered with his ability to perform in bed. But Rachel had assured him repeatedly that she understood and that they would work through it together.

He finished his lunch and returned to his office, a stately antebellum mansion on Adams Avenue, in an area of Memphis known as the Victorian Village. Most of the houses on the street were on the historical registry. This house was one of the oldest, with huge magnolia trees on the front lawn that were as old as the house itself. The main thing that distinguished it from the other antebellum homes was the large sign on the corner that read, "Law Offices of Marcus, Rosenberg, and Katz, LLC."

Sy entered through the back door, heading for the reception desk. The sweet, moon-faced receptionist, Annie, turned to see him coming and got up to hand him his messages. He snatched them from her outstretched hand as he headed toward the back stairs up to his office. He hated the old, narrow maid's staircase. He was exhausted, and the arthritis in his knees, with its gripping stiffness, was worse than usual today. Because the stairs were so steep, every step was agonizing, stretching his knees to their limit. *God, I'm getting old. I can't walk without pain. I can't read without glasses.* He stopped at the top of the stairs to catch his breath. His colleagues offered congratulations, which he tersely acknowledged. His secretary of twenty years, Dottie, in full makeup with rich red lips and every hair in place, handed him his mail and more messages. He took the papers from her, glancing through them as he spoke.

successful, it's because you have the clients with money. Your job is to confuse the jury, keep evidence out, and find a fall guy to create reasonable doubt. The 'truth' is what you can convince the jury to believe."

Marty, flustered, stared at Sy.

"And Marty, they're all innocent. Just ask them!"

Marty had slumped down in his chair and looked as if he had been slapped.

Sy took one look at him and realized he had overreacted. "Sorry, Marty; I'm just trying to protect you. I don't want you to have any false illusions about criminal law. It's a rough game out there. You will rarely represent an innocent man. You have to be cold and calculating, because your job is to act on behalf of your client's best interest. However, if possible, try to represent the white-collar criminals; they pay a lot better. Then you can afford to do pro bono work for the innocent victims. There are some, but most of them just can't afford a good attorney."

Sy moved forward, throwing his arms toward heaven, proclaiming, "Look; on my next big criminal trial, I'll have you assist me. You'll have a front-row seat on how to succeed as a criminal attorney. That will give you an insight on what you're getting into and, I hope, help you to make an informed choice on what type of law you want to practice."

Marty sat frozen in his chair. He then nodded and replied with a solemn "Thank you."

3

RACHEL WAITED ANXIOUSLY FOR SY TO PICK HER UP FOR THEIR appointment. She didn't like that she had to force Sy to go to the marriage counselor, but what else could she do? When she asked nicely, he ignored her. The tension between them had become unbearable. She could not understand why he had distanced himself from her. She wondered whether he was having an affair.

She stopped and looked in the mirror to check her hair. She had always taken pride in her appearance. She was slender, with a God-given lustrous complexion, and voluminous hair that was still its natural sable color—with a little help from Miss Clairol to cover the gray. Moreover, as a fashion designer, she generally dressed in one of her own designs. Today it was the bliss-blue tweed with long sleeves and patch-pocket jacket over a bliss-blue cotton/acrylic sheath with sheer yoke. She had attended to every detail, from her hairstyle to the designer shoes, to please her husband. She paced while waiting for him to pick her up, wringing her hands, her heart pounding as her mind raced. She walked into the sunroom, which overlooked a wooded area behind their home. It was a cloudy fall day, cold and dreary; but the birds were singing joyously, as if to proclaim a wondrous reprieve from a freeze the night before, which was unusually early for Memphis. As she looked at the forest below, a tree rained leaves all at once, as if someone had flipped a switch cutting off their life support. She watched as they tumbled to the ground. Rachel shivered, wondering whether it was an omen. Tears formed as she felt a deep sadness within. She jumped when the jarring honk of the horn signaled Sy's arrival.

She smiled as she got into the car and sat silent, waiting for a response from him. However, he remained intent on his driving, saying nothing to her until she could not take it anymore. Feeling rejected, she blurted out, "Are you angry with me for making you go to the therapist?"

Staring at the road ahead, he calmly stated, "No, honey, what's important to you is important to me." He then patted her hand and started talking about mundane things. Even though he felt manipulated by her divorce threats, he did realize the only remedy to get to and solve the problem was to ask the probing questions. Once she relaxed and was seemingly agreeable, he cautiously offered, "Rachel, honey, there's nothing wrong with our marriage. Do you think you're starting menopause? They say a lot of women go through it at your age."

Rachel bristled. "First, I'm on hormone therapy already. Second, hormones do not make you feel lonely and neglected. Third, why is it always my fault? I've begged you to plan a vacation with me; we both need a break. You don't come home for dinner anymore, and we never talk except to exchange messages. Whatever happened to you and to me, the way we used to be?"

Syrus went silent. Stonewalling was his usual tactic, which enraged Rachel. This was exactly why she needed an intermediary—someone to help her understand what he wanted, since he refused to talk to her about it. As he pulled into the parking lot of Dr. Schaffer's office, he remarked, "Well, maybe your doctor can tell me what to do to make you feel better." Rachel ignored him, and as soon as they entered the office, Sy became his "hail fellow well met" character, charming everyone, focusing special attention on the doctor.

In the session, Rachel did most of the talking, explaining to the doctor what a strong beginning they had, but how significant the change had become over the years, and that they had essentially lost their connection. Then she blatantly announced, "He's a workaholic; even when he's home, he's not there. If I try to talk to him, he acts as if I'm a nuisance. I feel so alone."

Sy was politely sitting in the meeting without comment. Dr. Schaffer turned and asked, "How do you feel about what your wife just said?"

He was quick to reply. "I know I work a lot, but I'm only doing it to make enough money so we can retire in style. I'm happy with Rachel and always have been. She's the perfect wife, lover, and mother of our children. There's nothing I would change."

Rachel moaned, "But you're never home, we rarely have dinner together anymore, and I feel abandoned."

Sy kindly told the doctor, "I really believe it's the empty nest syndrome. After all, both kids have gone off to college and I'm working as much as possible, but I have to strike while the iron's hot. I don't have that many years left to make the money to ensure a good retirement. Plus we have two kids in college, and even though we saved for their college, the cost of college has gone through the roof, so it's not enough."

Rachel shook her head while Sy continued to give his side of the story. Afterward the doctor responded, making suggestions and pointing out the simple things that could help their relationship. Sy was quick to apologize to Rachel and said he would make a concerted effort to be home for dinner at least three to four nights a week. He never mentioned their sex life.

By the time they left the doctor's office, Rachel had begun to believe maybe their problems were all in her head. Then Sy ever so sweetly proffered, "I don't see any need for me to go back, but if it makes you feel better, then you should see him." Gingerly, he grasped her hand. Grinning, he added, "Honey, I do think we need a vacation. I'll get you my schedule, and you figure out where we're going; but check with me before you book it, because court dates can change."

Rachel lit up with a big smile. *So, he was listening; he does want to work out our issues.* "That would be wonderful, darling. Nothing would make me feel better than some alone time with you on an island paradise."

Sy smiled lovingly and squeezed her hand. "Me too."

birthday dinner. Do you think she has any idea about Sammy's surprise party afterward? Have you heard anything?"

"*Kein ayin hara* [knock on wood], no one is talking, so she doesn't suspect a thing. For you, don't worry; Sammy is good at keeping secrets."

"Is Sammy coming to dinner tomorrow?"

"No, Hope said he has a container coming in from France and has to stay to oversee doing the inventory so his employees can't steal from him. I don't know why you girls can't get your husbands to come home for Shabbat dinner. Your father would never have missed being with his family on Shabbat. It was his joy in life."

"Yeah, you had an advantage; men had to eat at home because there were no fast-food drive-throughs, not to mention you keep kosher and Dad would never have eaten *treif*."

Sara's brow furrowed. "Syrus works too much; you need to put your foot down."

"You should live so long to see that. Sy claims he can't get any work done until everyone leaves the office and the phones stop ringing. He is by far the busiest attorney in his office, and he takes on too many cases."

"That's no excuse to miss Shabbat dinner," Sara growled. "It's only one night a week. The Torah says to remember the Sabbath and to keep it holy."

"Yeah, Mom, I know. Tell that to Sy."

"What is going on with your Sy? Something is different. He looked so run-down last time I saw him. Is he sick?"

"I don't know what's wrong. He has become even more of a workaholic since the kids left for college. He's not happy, but he won't talk to me about what's troubling him. Believe me; I've tried."

5

Sammy Grossman turned his car into the driveway leading to the parking lot of Lady Luck's Casino Hotel in Tunica, Mississippi. He looked around for the familiar car of Sharon Chambliss, the woman he was meeting. He was disappointed when he didn't see it and wondered if she had changed her mind or was just late as usual.

Sammy checked into the hotel, and the bellman asked if he could get his bag. "No, I'll take it myself," he replied, and he picked up the small duffel bag and headed for the elevator. As Sammy punched the elevator button, a skinny, dark-haired woman in a leather outfit and stiletto heels sidled up to him "Hey, handsome, want some company?"

Sammy laughed as he pushed Sharon into the elevator in front of him. "I like that outfit, hot stuff." He reached over and ran his hand up her leg and underneath her short skirt. As he reached her butt, he smiled and pulled her in close. He had pushed up the skirt far enough to see her bare ass, and he moaned. They stopped kissing and groping each other as the elevator slowed to a stop. Sammy and Sharon rushed to their room, and as soon as they were behind closed doors, they started peeling off their clothes.

The sun was setting outside the hotel room behind Sharon, who was dressed only in her leather outfit, complete with black leather boots adorned with sharp cone-shaped brass studs from the top of the boot to the toes. She laughed as she cracked her whip over Sammy, who lay face up with his taut ass gyrating while he tugged at his hands, which were tied to the headboard with scarves.

"You must grovel at my feet and obey my every demand!"

"I will. I'll do anything you ask, you nympho wench."

Sharon gleefully untied him. "Here's what I want." She straddled him and forced his throbbing erection inside her, her lips filled with hunger, vigorously kissing and biting him.

Minutes later Sammy was standing, buttoning his shirt, and putting on his suit pants. As he carefully tucked in his expensive Italian shirt and zipped up his pants, he nonchalantly inquired, "Are you going to the party tomorrow night?"

Sharon replied, "Now honey, you know I wouldn't miss Hope's birthday party for anything in the world. Why, she's one of my best friends." Sharon laughed heartily as Sammy slapped her on the ass.

6

Syrus was dressed in a tailored navy-blue suit with his favorite burgundy-and-silver tie, which was nicer than his usual attire for a Saturday. He had a late appointment at a lawyer's office downtown, so he had told Rachel he would meet them in the lobby of the Peabody Hotel. As he walked through downtown Memphis, he pondered his adopted city.

Memphis was a beautiful city with lots of southern charm, but it was its own worst enemy. Though it was referred to as the midsouth, it was more southern than most of the Deep South. Its residents were conservative and traditional, and they reveled in its past, when cotton was king and Memphis was its kingdom. Little had changed since its heyday in the early twentieth century. The bluebloods hung on desperately to what was, and the new blood kept fighting for change. Consequently, very little progress could be made, and the battle generally ended in stagnation, with the sultry, torrid climate perpetuating the impasse. Then, when winter did set in, it reminded them all that change was inevitable and often welcome. However, in the South, the winter is short and the long, sweltering summer soon returns, again heightening the tension as the South's need for the past to be ever present is played out and, once again, the past is exalted with glorified pilgrimages and Civil War battle reenactments.

As he walked in the stifling heat, Sy took off his suit coat. It was a typical Memphis-in-May evening; warm air hung heavily with humidity, so thick and sticky it seemed as if someone had poured honey on everything. The streets downtown were narrow, with most of the office buildings having been built in the early 1920s and '30s. Looking around, Sy chuckled. No matter what was happening in the rest of the world, downtown Memphis still reeked of the old South, with barbecue smell in the air, black singers belting out soulful songs from nearby blues clubs, and a horse and buggy clacking in tune on the concrete streets.

The historic Peabody Hotel, lavishly rebuilt in the 1920s after the original had burned to the ground, was the crown jewel of downtown. It was the ultimate place to have a glamorous dinner party, providing one could afford it; and for Sammy Grossman, no money would be spared to have a first-class celebration for his wife's birthday.

As Sy walked into the hotel, he spotted Rachel and their kids. Jason was a near clone of his father, and Mindy had inherited her mother's lustrous complexion but Sy's mother's Persian green eyes and wavy black hair. As he walked toward them, he was as jubilant as a child going to Disneyland, smiling and waving a jovial greeting. Rachel, with adoring eyes and a big grin, stood to greet him. He pulled her in close for a hug and then pulled away, looking her up and down; she wore a long red velvet gown that accentuated her voluptuous figure. "Wow, you are gorgeous!" His eyes filled with admiration. He raised his voice, motioning to their kids. "Shall we make our way to Aunt Hope's celebration?"

As they ascended the opulent staircase to the mezzanine, Sy took Rachel's hand, assuming the lead, as Jason and Mindy trailed behind them. They proceeded down the long hallway to the dining room where the celebratory dinner for Hope was being held.

Rachel was anxious to see the dining room. She hoped they had replicated her design. She had ordered the flowers, china, and crystal with very precise instructions. When she entered the room, she was delighted. Glittering chandeliers hung above the long table draped with a damask tablecloth beautifully adorned with tall, elegant crystal centerpieces topped in a lush array of roses and stargazer flowers in purples, reds, and greens. The table was just as Rachel had envisioned; there were settings fit for a queen with elaborate silver, gorgeous china, and multiple crystal goblets for every imaginable thirst.

As usual, Sara was in command of the intimate gathering, greeting the family as they entered. Even though she was a diminutive elderly woman, she directed the family gatherings as if she were a master sergeant.

Hope, already seated at the head of the table, rose to greet the family members as they entered the room. Sara pointed, directing her daughter, "Sit, sit; you can talk to them after we are all seated. Syrus, you sit here." She slapped the chair three down from the right side of the table. She then issued commands to everyone else where to sit, positioning herself between her two daughters.

Soon after, Sammy came rushing in, waving a small gift. "I'm so sorry, darling; I just couldn't get out of my business meeting as early as I planned."

Sara scowled as she directed him to his chair. "We know you're late. Sit, sit, so we can eat."

As they were nearing the end of their dinner, the waiter brought in coffee and a small birthday cake and lit the candles.

In unison, they all told Hope to make a wish before she blew out her candles, and then they joined in to sing "Happy Birthday to You."

Hope stood as she began her thanks. "First I want to thank everyone for being here. It means so much to me. I have already gotten everything I've wished for: to beat the cancer, to feel good again, and, most of all, to be here with y'all to celebrate my birthday. There were days when I thought I wouldn't be, but your love and support made all the difference in my belief that I could win the battle."

"Rachel, I owe you special thanks for always being there for me all hours of the day and night, and for taking me to the doctor and to my treatments when Sammy couldn't." She lifted her glass of wine, with

Hope laughed and turned to point. "My heavens, would you look at that cake? Why, it's bigger than my wedding cake."

Alfie, standing nearby, took this opportune moment to rush over and say, "I think it's time we cut the cake. How about it, birthday girl?"

Hope smiled broadly. "Yes, of course, Alfie."

Alfred hurriedly marched over to the bandstand and tapped on the microphone. "Excuse me please; may I have your attention? We'd like everyone to join us for the cutting of Hope's birthday cake."

Everyone moved toward her and began singing "Happy Birthday to You" as she cut the cake and gave the first piece to Sammy. Alfred handed her the microphone, and she thanked her husband for the party and then everyone else for being there, and she invited her guests to have cake and to take some home for their families. A server with small boxes had been set up at a table nearby to accommodate them taking the cake home.

As the party began to thin out, Rachel stood on one side of the room talking with friends while watching Sy, who was in an intense discussion with a group of men. She motioned across the room to him, signaling to meet her by the door where Hope and Sammy were thanking their guests as they left. Sy and Rachel approached them to say their goodbyes. By this time, the party had dwindled down to a small group.

Rachel gave Sammy a big hug. "Sammy, you've certainly lived up to your press clippings. The party was spectacular!"

Sy moved in and gave Hope a hug. "You're remarkable, Hope, for all you've been through; your courage has been an inspiration to all of us. My fondest wish is that we all will be together to celebrate your birthday for many more years."

Hope smiled. "You're such a love … I do wish you and Rachel would go with us to the Caribbean next month."

Rachel heard her and jumped in. "Oh, Syrus, let's go. We haven't been out of town together in forever."

"Yes, I know. I'm sorry, but I have so much to do to prepare for my big trial coming up in June. I wouldn't be able to relax or enjoy myself."

Sammy jumped in. "I have use of the Great Midwest corporate

yacht for two weeks. Alfred and Hope are going the first week. Why don't y'all fly down with me the second week? You could get away for four or five days, couldn't you?"

Sy frowned. "I'm not free to take off any time I want; I have client appointments and court dates that would be next to impossible to change. I won't get a day off until the courts close in August."

"Oh honey, we could fly out on Friday night and fly back the following Wednesday," Rachel pleaded. "You'd only miss a few days of work. Couldn't one of the other lawyers in the firm cover you for a few days?"

Sy turned on Rachel and, in a stern voice, curtly replied, "No, it's not a good time for me to leave." Feeling as if he had punched her in the stomach, Rachel shrank back with tears welling up in her eyes. Sammy quickly cut in, saying, "Well, if you change your mind, the price is right."

Sharon, who had been standing nearby, moved in close to Hope. "Hope, I would love to join you until Sammy gets there. Why, it'd be just like when we were at Vanderbilt having one of our all-night hen parties."

Hope smiled and hugged her. "Yes, wouldn't that be lovely."

Sy directed Rachel to the door.

Minutes later at the Peabody Hotel valet stand, Rachel stood silently as they waited for Sy's silver Lincoln to pull up. He could see by the scowl on Rachel's face that she was angry. She got in and slammed the car door before the valet could even get over to assist her.

As he pulled the car into the street, heading for home, he tried to placate her. "Sorry, Rach, but I can't take off right now. Why don't you go without me?"

"You told me to plan a vacation for us, and I told you about this trip two months ago, and you kept putting me off. The trip is only for five days."

"I told you I had a full court schedule and could not take off until the courts close in August."

"This is the third time I've tried to plan a vacation for us, but you always find a way out. Isn't it funny how you can always find four days to take off for the St. Jude Classic, but you can't find four days to spend with me?"

"It's once a year; I'm with you every day."

"You're with me every day? We barely speak except to give each other messages. You're always at the office late."

"For God's sake, Rachel, I'm working."

"That's always your excuse. Look at the sleazy clients you're representing. When you started out in the prosecutor's office, you cared about upholding the law and defending the innocent. What happened to that man?"

"I chose to make money so we could have all the things we wanted. What the hell do you want now? You have everything!"

"I want you again … I feel like I'm living alone."

"Wait a minute. You wanted the big house, the private schools, your own business; I gave you all that and more. So now, suddenly, you want to change the rules on me."

"You're missing the issue. I appreciate and value all the things we have, but I want more time with you, the way we used to be."

"Yeah, sure, ever since the kids left for college, you've been depressed and moody. You're having the empty nest syndrome."

"Oh, that's great! Make it sound like the problem is all mine and none of it is yours. I swear men do not see the writing on the wall until it's on a court document. Is that where we're headed, Sy?"

Sy sneered, "What's gotten into you?"

A dead silence ensued for the remainder of the trip home.

As Sy pulled into the driveway of their stately Georgian home, he tried to pretend that nothing was wrong.

"What time did you tell the kids to be home?"

Rachel shook her head as she cried out, "You haven't heard a word I've said, have you?"

Sy went silent as Rachel got out of the car and slammed the door. He stayed in the car for a while to calm down.

Tears flowed down Rachel's cheeks as she walked into the guest bedroom, closed the door, and flung herself on the bed, burying her sobs in the pillow. *I just do not understand why I can't get through to him,* she thought. All he had done after seeing the therapist, was to say she should plan a vacation for them. *But obviously that was only to appease me*, she reasoned, *and get me off his back; he didn't mean a word of it.* Their fights were happening more and more. *What is wrong with me? Am I asking too much for him to take a few days off work?* Then her mind darted to a possibility she didn't want to consider: was he having an affair? *Why did he stop loving me? What did I do that was so wrong?* She sat up and took a deep breath. She had to get out of her pity party; the kids would be home soon. She had to pull herself together and put on a brave front for them. She didn't want the kids going back to college worried that their parents were getting a divorce. She got up and went into the bathroom to wipe off the smeared makeup and put a pretend smile on her face. She could go into the den and watch TV until the kids returned home, and by then Sy would be asleep and she could go to bed.

7

THE MORNING SUN REFLECTED OFF THE MISSISSIPPI RIVER AS A HUGE barge moved slowly down river. Sammy was driving his white Cadillac down Riverside Drive while Hope applied lipstick in her visor mirror.

Hope sighed, "Did the police say if anyone had broken in?"

"No, but the neighborhood is going from bad to worse, and everyone knows I have a warehouse full of liquor," Sammy answered gruffly. "I need to install cameras and a monitor, because while the security guard is on one side of the building, robbers could break in on the other side—one more huge expense."

He pulled the car up next to the police car parked in front of the warehouse. The alarm was blaring. Sammy got out of the car to greet the police officer and security guard. He quickly unlocked the door and motioned them inside. Hope stayed in the car. Finally, the alarm went silent. Soon after Sammy and the men exited the building, Sammy locked up as the police officer and guard checked the outside of the building. Sammy thanked them as he got back into his car. He started the car and slammed it into gear.

"It was nothing. That crazy alarm went off by itself again."

"Well, I'm glad nothing's wrong."

Sammy checked his rearview mirror as he headed back down Riverside Drive. Hope stared out the window at the river. As they stopped for a light, Hope noticed a man standing at the edge of the water, removing his wallet, wedding ring, and shoes. As she was trying to decide what was unusual about the way he stood there, he walked straight into the river and disappeared.

"Oh my God! Sammy, pull over; that man is drowning!"

Sammy pulled into the parking lot and stopped at the edge of the levee. Hope jumped out of the car, ran across a plank onto a paddlewheel boat, grabbed a life preserver, and dove into the current, swimming toward the drowning man. Sammy quickly called 911 on his car phone before running down to the water, yelling, "Help! Help me! My wife's in the river."

Two men came out from the paddlewheel boat to see what all the commotion was. Sammy pointed at the drowning man and Hope. They quickly grabbed a long pole to help pull the two of them to shore and then waded into the water and helped both of them to the shore. Another dockworker from nearby brought blankets and wrapped one around Hope. "Are you crazy, lady? You could have drowned!"

Hope was more concerned with the man she had pulled out of the water. As he coughed and gagged, Hope moved over to him and spoke in a soothing, sweet voice.

"You're going to be all right."

He focused his eyes on her in disdain. "Why couldn't you just let me die?"

"No matter how bad things may seem, there's always another option."

"I've used up all my options; anything would be better than my life."

"It wasn't your time or I wouldn't have been here to save you. Things will get better; you'll see. There are lots of people who will help you."

"Who are you? What's your name?"

"Hope."

The man began to sob as he buried his face in the blanket. Hope tried to comfort him. The police asked her to step over to their car so they could get her statement. Sammy walked toward them as she explained what had transpired. With a scowl, Sammy pointed at his watch. The paramedics arrived and began loading the man into the ambulance. Hope rushed over to them. "What hospital are you taking him to?"

"Mercy General on Jefferson."

Hope patted the man's foot. "Don't worry about anything. I'll be over to see you as soon as I can."

Sammy barked, "Let's go! I have things to do; I need to get home." He turned and started walking back to the car. Hope ran to catch up with him.

Back at home, Hope cleaned up, dried her hair, and then headed for the hospital. As soon as she returned, Sammy asked her to fix lunch. He had managed to track down Alfie, who was coming over to discuss the alarm incident. She made sandwiches, and just as she finished putting side dishes and chips on the table, the doorbell rang. She opened the door to greet Alfie.

"Hope, I just heard your name on the radio; you're a hero! Did you really pull that man out of the Mississippi?"

"Well, I couldn't just watch him drown. I was a lifeguard. Now how would that have looked?"

"I guess, but I couldn't have saved him; I wear water wings in the bathtub."

Hope broke out in laughter as Sammy joined them in the hallway.

"Where the hell were you this morning when the alarm went off?"

"I was having brunch with some friends." Alfie put his hand to his mouth and whispered to Hope, "I see he's in his usual chipper mood."

Sammy turned on his heels and yelled, "Come on in the kitchen."

Hope turned and went upstairs to her room. When she entered her bedroom, she picked up the book she had been reading the night before and went outside to the deck that overlooked the pool and the beautiful landscaped backyard. She settled into the chaise longue, enjoying the remnants of the cooler morning air, and began to read. Her serenity was abruptly interrupted by Sammy's angry ranting. She looked over the side to see Sammy and Alfie outside the office of the old guesthouse at the far left side of the pool area. Sammy was angrily waving some papers as he chided Alfie.

"What is this? I got a bill for solid wood interior doors. For Christ's sake, we're not building the Taj Mahal, and we're not in a position to spend money on luxuries like this."

"It gives them class and cuts down on the noise. It's a great selling feature."

"Not if we're bankrupt before they're finished. We're four months behind on the payments and a million dollars over budget!"

Hope watched Alfie bow his head, blinking back tears as he stared at the ground. She was sure he was wishing that somehow the earth would open up and swallow him.

Sammy grasped Alfie's shoulder to get his attention and shook him as he fervently warned him, "Listen to me; you do your part, and I'll do mine. If we can just hold the bank off a little longer, we can get this worked out. But no more frivolous spending. We do not have the money to pay this. Do you understand?" Sammy released his shoulder and ran his hand slowly down Alfie's arm as he lifted his chin up to look into his eyes. Alfie beamed as he leaned into him. Sammy smiled and took Alfred's hand and led him into their office.

Hope's suspicions that they were intimately involved sickened her. She quickly turned away, slipping quietly back into the house, hoping they hadn't noticed her. Was it possible Sammy was gay, or was he placating Alfie? That's what Sammy had said when she confronted him about his relationship with Alfie. If only she could understand what was going on between them. She only knew that a huge wedge had wriggled its way into her and Sammy's relationship.

Hope had always wondered whether Sammy's relationship with his mother was to blame, although Sammy worked for his father in the family business. Sammy's mother, Naomi, had been the bookkeeper for the company. She had an opinion about everything Sammy did, usually to criticize. These criticisms were always followed by her saying they were to help him be a better man. While her husband, Alvin, ran

wedding next week, and I've designed all the bridesmaids' gowns as well as the wedding gown. I'll probably need to be there right up to the moment they walk down the aisle."

Rachel pulled into the driveway of Hope's home. Hope said, "I know you need to go, but I need your advice on something; it'll just take a few minutes."

Rachel nodded.

"I overheard Sammy talking to Alfred, saying they were four months behind on their payments on the brownstone project. I don't know how much the payments are, but surely the bank will be making demands soon."

Rachel cried out, "Four months? You're damn right the bank will be doing something soon. Did Sammy ask you for your inheritance money?"

"No, so maybe he's got a plan in place to cover it. He never talks to me about our finances, so I'm not sure what to do. I wanted to keep the money for when I file for divorce, but then again I want to get the brownstones finished."

"Hope, you know Sy and I would give you and Sammy a loan. And I'm sure Mom would help. Uncle Stanley would help too. We're not going to let you and Sammy lose everything. We just may end up owning part of the deal. Tell Sammy we'll help."

Hope felt relieved. "Oh my gosh, that would be so helpful. I'll tell him and let you know what he says. Hope sighed as she shook her head. "You know, Rach, I really don't want to go on this trip with Sammy, but he's made such a big deal out of it being for our anniversary that I don't know how to get out of it. And he's been so attentive lately with the birthday party and all; I don't know what to think."

"Are you still planning on leaving Sammy when you get back from the trip?"

"Most likely," Hope said. "You know Sammy: one week he loves me dearly, and the next week he acts as if I am the bane of his existence. I really thought the brownstones would be finished by now, so I'm hoping Sammy will tell me about it when we're together on the trip. I'll use your offer of financial support to try to get him to talk about it with me. But if he erects that impenetrable armor of silence again, I will definitely leave him when we return. I'd rather die than keep living like this."

Rachel reached over and gave her a reassuring hug. "You know I'm always here for you, and I understand how hard this is for you." Cheerfully, she stated, "However, tonight we're going to celebrate in style and have a great send-off for you and Sammy."

"Okay, see you then." Hope, smiling, got out of the car.

Later that evening, Rachel and Sy arrived at the restaurant while the sun was still setting. The striking orange-and-gold sunset matched the jovial, noisy crowd of the restaurant where Hope and Sammy were already seated. Sammy saw them coming and motioned to the waiter to order a round of drinks for everyone. As soon as Rachel sat down, she started talking to Hope, as if they hadn't been together in days.

After a wonderful dinner and a few glasses of wine, Rachel blurted out, "Wow, I still can't believe you jumped in the Mississippi to save that guy. You could have drowned! Then where would I be, you little twit?"

"I wouldn't have drowned; I grabbed a life preserver before I jumped. Besides, when it's your time to go, it's your time, and it wasn't Wendell's time to go—and thankfully not my time either."

Sy leaned in and said, "Yes, but it's awfully risky to jump into the raging Mississippi this time of year, even though what you did was very courageous."

"Well, he was close to the shore. Besides, courage is having no fear, and after what I've been through, I've made peace with the fear of death. It's just a transition to the other side."

Sy sat back and took a gulp of his drink. "You really believe that? That dying is just a transition?"

"Yes, that's what the Torah says. Why, what do you think happens when you die?"

"You cease to exist; you're dead. It's dark. You're in the ground."

"That's awfully final, Sy. Every religion believes the soul lives on. Even pagans believe in an afterlife."

"Promising eternal life is just organized religion's way of controlling people's lives and their money. Isn't that right, Sammy?"

Sammy laughed. "Yeah, that eternal life crap is a big moneymaker."

"Right, Sammy; the only thing we know for sure is there's a now and you'd better make the most of it."

Rachel chimed in. "Hey, hey, hey, this is supposed to be a bon voyage party. Let's celebrate!" She lifted her glass in salutation, "L'chayim!"

They all joined in with a salute to life. They ordered coffee and dessert as the men's conversation drifted back into Sammy's latest ventures in the import business and Sy's demanding schedule with the deluge of white-collar criminals. Hope and Rachel's conversation was concerning Hope's impending future as a grandmother. Rachel was glad to see Hope happier than she had been since her cancer battle began. As the evening descended into darkness, not one of them wanted to end the party. When they did leave the restaurant, Rachel and Hope lingered outside on the sidewalk, saying their goodbyes.

As Sy and Rachel turned to walk back to the car, Rachel turned to look at Hope walking away in the distance, and an agonizing melancholy came over her. Feeling shaky and inebriated, she reached out to hold on to Sy. He pulled her in close and looked at her curiously. "Are you feeling okay? You can't possibly be cold; it's ninety-eight degrees out."

Rachel collapsed into his embrace. "I don't feel very good. I hope I'm not getting that summer flu bug that's going around."

He looked lovingly into her sad azure eyes. "If you're not feeling better in the morning, you'd better see a doctor right away. You need to nip it in the bud."

"Yes, you're right. I'll call if I don't feel better." This brief display of warmth from Sy was such a relief that she momentarily forgot how chilly it had been between them. She wanted to bring up the subject of planning a vacation for the two of them in August but decided it was still a touchy subject, so she didn't. Besides, all she wanted now was to get home and go to bed. She'd had too much to drink, and the drinking had intensified those old feelings of dread that were still taking a toll on her.

The next morning, after a fitful night of sleep, Rachel awakened and remembered a dream that was particularly vivid. She had walked into a house—a house that seemed familiar, but she did not know whose house it was. Several mirrors were covered in black cloth. This was a Jewish tradition in which, from the time of death to the end of sitting shiva—the seven days of mourning following the burial—one covers all mirrors in the house because vanity has no place in a house of mourning. However, in Rachel's dream, as she looked at the mirrors, she heard a voice behind her say, "The divine image that you reflect is not one that can be seen with the eyes." She remembered a day in her Torah study class when they had discussed at length the subject of covering the mirrors with a black cloth. The class determined that the concept had more to do with remembering our divine image and recognizing that it is much more significant than our mortal image, which is our primary focus. They noted that nothing makes one more aware of one's own mortality and more hopeful of one's *immortality* than the death of someone a person loves and reveres, which leaves that person hanging onto the frantic hope that they will get to see and be with that person again.

The dream haunted her for the rest of the day.

9

June 19, 1993

HOPE GOT OUT OF BED, PULLED ON A ROBE, AND MADE HER WAY TO the galley. It was a dark and tumultuous morning on the Caribbean Sea with threatening gray clouds that rumbled perilously.

As she looked out over the water, all she could see were dark gray clouds. Hope felt the gloom engulfing the yacht intensifying her depression. She was angry with herself for even agreeing to go on this trip when she really wanted to stay home. She could not believe that after twenty-eight years she still couldn't stand up to Sammy and say what she wanted. The yacht was bobbing on the water like a toy boat, and her stomach bobbed along with it, making her nauseated. She had taken Dramamine before she left her room, but it didn't seem to be helping. Sharon was already making coffee in the galley when Hope entered.

"Good morning. How did you sleep last night?" Sharon laughed. "After listening to Alfie drone on about wonderful Sammy, that boring drivel made me so sleepy that as soon as my head hit the pillow, I was out. We should record him and sell it as a sleeping aid." Both women laughed.

"Sharon, would you mind handing me my pills? They're in the cabinet right above your head."

"Oh, sure." Sharon brought them to Hope. By then the coffee was ready, and she poured each of them a cup before sitting down at the table. Hope sat and talked with Sharon for over fifteen minutes, hoping the Dramamine would kick in. She got up to put a bagel in the toaster.

Sharon's eyes were darting from door to door as if she were expecting someone. With a crooked smile, she said, "Hope, I need to pack and get ready so I can get to the airport in time to catch my flight. How long do you think it'll take for the yacht to get to the island?"

Hope was standing near the toaster, waiting for it to pop up. She turned around to answer her. "It shouldn't take more than an hour and a half. I'm so seasick I think I'm going to stay on the island and let the boys go out on the yacht by themselves. You sure you don't want to stay with me on the island?"

"Oh, I wish I could, but I have to get back to work, and right now I'd better get back to my room to pack; it'll take more than an hour for me to get ready."

Hope smiled. "Okay." She watched as Sharon left, grasping the railing while carefully balancing her cup of coffee. Hope slathered cream cheese on her bagel and sat down to take a bite, hoping she could keep it down. As she was getting her pills out and putting them in the saucer with her coffee, Alfie appeared in the doorway. He made his way to the booth and slumped into the seat next to her, groaning.

"I am so hungover. Hope, would you be a darling and pour me some coffee?"

Hope sullenly poured Alfie a cup of coffee and sat back in the booth with him. As she slathered her bagel with more cream cheese, she commented, "Quite a storm we had last night, huh?"

Alfie moaned, "Is that what that was? I thought it was just the hangover that was making me sick."

She took a bite of her bagel and then downed a few of the pills with her coffee. As she took another bite, she began to gag.

Alfie jumped up to help. "Are you okay?"

"I'm fine; I'm fine." Hope waved him away, gripped by a roiling in her stomach. She made her way into the head a few steps away and shut the door behind her.

Alfie heard her cough and gag. After a few moments, it was quiet. Then he heard a thud from within the bathroom. He jumped up and pounded frantically on the door. "Hope—Hope, are you okay? Answer me."

When he didn't get a response, he tried to open the door, but it wouldn't open. He ran onto the deck screaming for someone to help him. Two crewmembers joined him, and together they tried to force the door open. One of them slammed into the door with all his might. It took two more tries before he could break it up enough to pull Hope's body out of the bathroom, lay her on the galley floor, and start CPR.

By now everyone on the yacht had heard the commotion and was coming to see what had happened. The ship's captain brought a defibrillator; after several tries, he gave up and pronounced her dead. Alfie screamed and cried, "Oh my God! She can't be dead. It's not possible. Sammy will just be destroyed." Alfie lifted her hand and kissed it, crying woefully. "Oh my God, how will I tell him?" He clung to her hand, sobbing. Sharon stepped forward and hugged Alfie, crying with him, trying to console him as best she could.

The captain announced they would leave immediately for Bimini, the nearest island, to report the incident to the authorities. As soon as they were allowed off the boat, Alfie called Sammy to tell him what had happened.

Sammy cried silently and said, "Do not let them do an autopsy; it's against Jewish law. Do not let them touch her, please. Stay with the body. Have them call me as soon as possible; I must talk to them. And get her jewelry off her right now, before someone decides to make it disappear. Please, Alfie, help me with this. I'll fly there if I have to."

"It's going to be fine, Sammy; I can handle this. I will talk to them and call you right after so we can decide what to do about the body and how to get her back home to Memphis, okay?"

"Okay, but I need to talk to them as soon as possible."

10

RACHEL WALKED OUT TO THE DRIVEWAY IN THE EARLY MORNING TO retrieve the newspaper. *What a gorgeous day, no rain, no humidity, and no wind*—so *not Memphis in June.* She noticed the stillness; it was too calm, like the calm before a storm. Panic surged deep within her. She didn't know why; she just sensed that something was wrong. When she walked back into the house, she chided herself. *How silly it is of me to turn a perfectly beautiful day into* a *sinister event.* She laid the paper down to pour a cup of coffee. She could hear Sy talking on the phone in the den, so she poured only one cup. She would pour his when he joined her. She had opened to the arts and culture section of the newspaper when Sy walked into the kitchen. She glanced up to see him staring at her. He looked stricken, his eyes brimming with tears.

"Sy, what's wrong?"

"It's Hope, Rachel."

She felt a stab in the pit of her stomach. Sy walked over to her, pulled her from the chair, and held her close. "I'm sorry, honey, but Hope has died."

Rachel pulled back and stared at him in disbelief. She tried to speak but could not form words. She could not breathe. She was sure she had not heard him right; her sister couldn't be dead. She was fine; she was on a trip in the Caribbean, and her husband was flying down to join her today. She had just spoken with Hope a few days prior, and she had been fine.

"I just got off the phone with Sammy. He was getting ready to leave for the airport when he got the call. Apparently she choked to death this morning while eating breakfast."

Rachel pulled away from Sy, trembling and crying. "It can't be true, Sy; it just can't be true."

"I'm sorry, darling; I'm afraid it is."

She cried out, "Oh God, please don't let this be true." Sy held her close and let her cry for a while before gently saying, "Honey, Sammy wants us to go over and tell your mother. I know it won't be easy, but we have to do it."

Rachel crumpled to the floor, wailing, "Oh my God, this can't be happening, this can't be happening! How are we going to tell Mom? This could kill her; her heart can't take it." She felt as if she had fallen into a black hole. She could not feel her body or move it. The pain was crushing, and she could barely breathe.

Sy pulled her up off the floor and held her tightly, speaking softly. "I'll handle it. Please, Rachel, go get dressed. We need to get over to your mother's before she hears it from someone else."

"Yes, yes, we need to get over to Mom's." She sobbed as she made her way to the bedroom. She blindly grabbed a pair of jeans and top, shaking so badly she could barely get her clothes on. Only her brain functioned; her heart had been forsaken. A huge part of her life had been taken away, and nothing could ever replace it.

11

THE FUNERAL WAS A TRIBUTE OF ADORATION FROM HOPE'S FAMILY AND friends, with an overflowing crowd that the tiny chapel at the Jewish cemetery could not accommodate.

Afterward everyone made their way to Sammy and Hope's home, where they would be sitting shiva, the traditional seven days of mourning.

It was a crowd of well over two hundred people. It included friends from the symphony orchestra, which she had been an important part of, as well as colleagues from the JCC and St. Jude Hospital, where she had volunteered through the years.

Their house was a turn-of-the-century mansion with several large rooms on the first floor. Fresh flowers were everywhere. The mirrors were covered in black cloth, and every table, large or small, was laden with food. In true southern fashion, Sammy had the servants dressed in crisp black-and-white uniforms with white gloves. Several of them scurried around picking up dishes and replenishing the food as soon as it disappeared.

When Rachel walked into the house, she was instantly drawn to the mirrors covered in black cloth. She remembered the dream she'd had. Was it a precognition of Hope's death? Rachel joined the family gathered around her mother, Sara. Sy immediately went to the bar in the Florida room at the back of the house.

Sy stood sipping his drink as he gazed through the wall of glass at the well-appointed landscaping around the pool. Rabbi Levy, who had known the family forever, approached him and rested his hand on Sy's shoulder while expressing his condolences.

Slumped in despair with teary red eyes, Sy turned to him. "I don't get it, Rabbi. If there were a God, why would he take someone like Hope and leave the murderers and child molesters here? Why not take them?"

The rabbi replied, "That is the question of the ages—one I don't know the answer to. I understand your feelings, and I know that Hope will be sorely missed, but she is with Hashem in a better place. She—"

Sy stiffened defiantly and sputtered, "Really, you expect me to believe Hope's in a better place? Dead in the ground?"

"Have faith that her soul is with Hashem. Only her body—"

Syrus again cut him off. "Faith. Nice pat answer to everything y'all can't answer or explain."

The rabbi patiently replied, "Faith is a treasure that can be neither questioned nor fully explained—not unlike your soul."

"Excuse me." Sy quickly turned his back on him and headed back to the bar for a refill.

Alfie was talking with Diane. He looked up to see Rachel approaching them as he said, "I felt so helpless. I wish there were more I could have done to save your mother."

Rachel butted in. "Excuse me, Alfred; there's something I don't understand. If she was obviously choking, why in the world did you let her go into the bathroom alone?"

Alfie looked stricken and mumbled, "I don't know; it happened so fast, and she pushed me away and went into the bathroom and closed the door."

Rachel's uncle tapped her on the shoulder and motioned for her to come with him. Her mother, Sara, sat on the sofa holding a picture of

Hope with Diane as a baby. She cried out to God, "I'm old; why couldn't he have taken me? Why would he take my Hope? Why would he make me bury my baby?"

Everyone around her was trying to console her, but no one could. Rachel moved in next to her and held her mother in her arms, crying with her. From out of the blue, a picture inexplicably fell from the fireplace mantle, shattering the glass and startling everyone nearby. Rachel quickly moved to pick it up; it was a picture of Hope and Sammy. A woman standing close by asked, "What happened?"

Rachel shook her head. "I don't know; maybe it was pushed too close to the edge."

Rachel went to find Sammy to have him get someone to sweep up the glass. He stood near the grand piano, surrounded by people trying to comfort him. He cried out dramatically, "What will I do without my beloved Hope? My only solace is knowing that she is still with us in spirit." Alfie moved in to hold him as he sobbed. Rachel glared at them with contempt and went to ask a servant to clean up the glass. She just could not deal with Sammy in this moment. An intuitive feeling told her he was overplaying his grief and loving all the attention, but then Rachel was so confused she wasn't sure she could figure out what anything meant anymore. Nothing made sense, nothing would ever be the same again, and all she knew was that she was numb with pain. *I have to stay strong. I have to get Mom through this, and I have to be strong for Diane and get her through her pregnancy. I have to be strong for everyone, just as I have always done.* She had always been the tower of strength in the family; she couldn't bail on them now, when they needed her the most. But for the first time in her life, Rachel didn't feel she had the strength to carry on. Now she had no one to lean on. She was sure that after shiva ended, everyone's life would go back to normal except for Diane's, her mother's, and hers.

For so many days after the funeral, Rachel felt as if she were sleepwalking through the day. Hope's death had condensed time into a meaningless blur. The depression was so bad on some days that she couldn't eat or sleep, and tears constantly welled up, making it hard for her to draw a design, sew, or even think. She felt as if someone had cut out her heart and used it for a football, kicking it and laughing gleefully as she cried out in agony. She simply could not function, and for the first time in her life, suicide did sound painless. But she knew she had to push through those feelings. Her mother needed her more than ever, and so did Diane. Still Rachel felt so alone because, once Shiva ended, Sy was nowhere to be found.

Life had a way of moving her into the demands of the day, and she had no choice as she was forced to get back to the here and now. She returned to the office, where she focused on her clients' needs because it helped to keep the depression at bay. Today was going to be better but still hard; Diane was coming into the shop to see her. She was going to give her Hope's jewelry that had been kept in Rachel's office safe.

Diane pulled into the parking lot and gingerly emerged from behind the steering wheel, protecting the new life of which she was the guardian. The sun was shining on the morning dew, sparkling like jewels in the swirling leaves. Seeing Diane full of life and knowing how much she was loved brought a smile to Rachel's face. Diane and Rachel had grown closer since Hope's death. They talked on the phone most days, and Rachel attended Lamaze classes with Diane when her husband could not make it. Rachel was thrilled when they told her they were going to name the baby Hope if it was a girl.

Rachel opened the door to greet her. "Diane, you look radiant."

"Thanks, Aunt Rachel. It's always good to look better than you feel, because I feel big as a barn." Both laughed as Rachel motioned her to the office in the back of the showroom. The jewelry was in a velvet bag already lying on the desk. Rachel pulled the chair out for her.

Rachel picked up the velvet bag and handed it to Diane. "This is all the jewelry that was in my safe. Your dad has the other pieces that were in the will. Has he given you your mother's diamond wedding ring?"

"No, he said he's just not ready yet, but he already gave me most of the other jewelry." Diane took the white pearl necklace out of the bag and started to tear up as she looked at it. "Momma's pearls ... I can see her in them. I miss her so much."

Fighting back her own tears, Rachel said, "I know. There isn't a day goes by that I don't miss her so much that my heart aches. Life will never be the same for any of us; she was such a love." Diane pulled out the rest of the jewelry. As she looked over each piece, she cried softly and then gently put them back in the bag.

When Diane rose from the chair to leave, Rachel went to her side and hugged her. Diane hugged her in return, and they supported each other as they made their way to the front door.

Rachel watched as Diane drove away, and she questioned how God could have taken Hope away right before she was going to experience the joy of having a grandchild. She wondered for the hundredth time whether there really was a God, and if so, what kind of being was this God. The anger welled up again. She had to stop thinking those thoughts or they would make her crazy. She had to let it go and somehow move on with her life.

12

FEELING ABANDONED BY SY, RACHEL AGONIZED OVER THE PROBLEMS in her marriage. Everyone always told her she was a worrywart, but she couldn't stop herself even though she was making herself a nervous wreck. Her daughter, Mindy, noticed. She said, "Mom, you keep telling me the same thing over and over. I get it, so stop worrying." The death of her sister had exaggerated her feelings of loss. Now, more than ever, she feared the loss of Syrus. In desperation, Rachel called and made an appointment with Dr. Schaffer.

When invited into his office, she picked the chair farthest from the north wall—the wall that was floor-to-ceiling bookcases, which were filled with books interspersed with dead animals. He had a stuffed armadillo, a huge dead (she hoped) tarantula, and one was a lifelike (maybe stuffed; she wasn't going to touch it to find out) bat with a snarling stare. She moved her chair so her back was to the wall of dead animals before saying, "I apologize for not coming back sooner, and Lord knows I need your help. I can't sleep or eat, because as you know, my sister died. Losing her has nearly destroyed me. If I lost Sy too, I don't know how I could handle it. For a while, he started coming home for dinner more often, but now he's not making any effort at all—probably because I'm so depressed and cry on a whim, but I can't help myself. My sister was the one person I could talk to about my feelings, and now I have no one."

The doctor sat patiently listening, his leathery liver-spotted hands propped on the desk, writing as he took notice about her concerns.

Dr. Schaffer looked like a throwback from the fourteenth century, with a long, straggly gray beard and long, sparse gray hair at the base of his skull. Nodding, he said, "Yes, I understand."

With tears in her eyes, she blurted out, "How does a love that starts out so strong, so right, change so drastically? Syrus and I started out so much in love. We dated for over five years before we married. We had the most idyllic start in life that anyone could hope to have. I just don't know what happened that changed everything so much. I have to pry a conversation out of Syrus, and it makes me feel like I am bothering him—like it's an imposition to have to pay attention to me."

The doctor shifted in his chair and in a quiet but clear voice said, "Besides his lack of communication, tell me what other problems concern you about your relationship with Syrus."

"Well, to start with, he will not come back with me for counseling because he says we don't have a problem; I'm the only one with a problem. He says I'm perfect, but he doesn't give me the time of day. I could be making love to another man in the middle of the living room floor, and he wouldn't say, 'Why are you naked?' or 'What's that man doing on top of you?' because he doesn't even look at me when he talks to me. It's like I'm invisible. When I try to talk to him about what's going on in his law practice, he gives me a two-word answer and acts like that's a bother."

Dr. Schaffer straightened in his chair, nodding, "When was the last time you felt any connection with your husband?"

She had to go back in time to recall. "I'd say it was four years ago, when we went on a trip for an educational seminar with the Trial Lawyers Association. The seminar was in Trinidad. We had a wonderful time. We talked and made love. It was paradise."

"Was that the last time you took a vacation together?"

"Yes."

"Why haven't you planned another vacation?"

"Therein lies the problem. Sy is always working. He works until nine or ten every night and most Saturdays. He claims he wants to make as much money as possible so we can have a nice retirement. He did say for me to plan a vacation for us, but every time I've tried, he's had an excuse for why we can't go. Plus, there are other things that worry me."

The doctor shifted in his chair and started writing. "What other things worry you?"

"He's so distant with me. We never hug or cuddle anymore like we used to."

Dr. Schaffer put his pen down and nodded thoughtfully. "How is the intimacy between you and your husband?"

"That's been an issue too. Sy has high blood pressure, and the doctor put him on a pill that made him impotent. He complained to the doctor, and he is trying a different medication, but he's still having problems. I wonder if he is just not attracted to me or, worse yet, if he's having an affair and faking this problem as an excuse to avoid me."

"Do you have any other reason for suspecting he's having an affair?"

"Well, he never comes home until late, and he either works or plays golf on Saturday—although I work every Saturday, so I don't know what he's up to. I did look at his car phone bill that was on his desk. There was nothing out of the ordinary on it, but he is smart enough not to leave a trail. After all, he is a criminal attorney."

"So you don't trust him?"

"No, I wouldn't say that. I would say I don't respect him as much anymore and I really don't believe he cares about me one iota. Two years ago, they found a lump in my breast and I had to go in for a biopsy. The doctor told me that if they found cancer, they would go ahead and take all of the breast tissue. I could have woken up to a death sentence. I was scared, but he couldn't take me to the hospital because he had to be in court. My sister took me. When I awoke, my sister and mother were the only ones there for me. He didn't even call until much later in the day to see what the outcome was. Does that sound like someone who cares?"

"What was the result of the biopsy?"

"Fortunately, it was benign."

"Did you say anything to him about your fear before the surgery?"

"Yes. He said he knew it was nothing to worry about and I would be okay. But that wasn't how I felt about it. My feelings didn't even register with him."

"So has Syrus mentioned getting a divorce?"

"No, but when I've mentioned it, he's ignored me and acted as if it's some kind of silly notion not worthy of his attention."

"He doesn't say anything?"

"Yes, he says, 'Kvetch, kvetch, kvetch' … which means 'Bitch, bitch, bitch.'"

"Yes, I know what it means. It sounds like you are not communicating with each other on any level. Has this always been an issue?"

"No. In the beginning, one of the reasons I was most fiercely attracted to him was the way we could talk about anything and everything. He always wanted to hear my opinion, even when he didn't agree. We were so in sync then. We had the most amazing beginning; I was sure nothing could ever tear us apart."

"What was so amazing?"

"The way we met … the experiences we shared in the beginning."

"Tell me how you met and what specific experiences you shared."

13

RACHEL LOVED TO TELL THEIR STORY. IT REMINDED HER OF HOW special their relationship was from the beginning.

"It was 1963, and I was in my first year at the University of Tennessee. At that time, it was one of the first southern colleges that admitted black students, albeit very few, before it became mandatory. One of my best friends was Eleanor, the daughter of Yolanda, our black maid. My mother, a college professor with connections, saw to it that Eleanor attended college alongside me. My mother believed in and promoted equality long before it became the law. She had always taught us kids that we were no better than anyone else and no one was better than we were. She always said everyone's heart was the same color and the heart was the only way you could judge someone, which you could see by how they lived their life, their kindness to others, and whether or not they helped those less fortunate."

"Anyway, my parents lived their lives by example. They should both be sainted; they were that good."

Dr. Schaffer nodded. "So you met in college?"

"Yes, by the end of Eleanor's and my first year at UT, the most exciting happening on campus was the talk about the march on

Washington, which was planned for August. It was a march for jobs and freedom, but it was also the centennial celebration of the signing of the Emancipation Proclamation. Several of the students in the Jewish fraternity wanted to be involved. They had announced that it was an open meeting for anyone interested, so Eleanor and I attended the meeting. The speaker was Syrus. He was imploring everyone there to join in the fight for justice and equality for all men and women, regardless of race or religion. His talking point was 'injustice is still injustice,' and I was intrigued by his speech and his persona. And he was so handsome in an unusual way. He had intense dark eyes, and thick, curly black ringlets falling around his face that made him look like a Greek god. Plus, he had a body to match, and I was smitten. Eleanor and I stayed after the meeting so we could talk to him. We asked him about riding on the buses that would be leaving from Memphis to go to Washington, DC. He immediately started telling us about all the possible perils of riding on the buses. He was talking to Eleanor, but then, in the middle of a sentence, Syrus stopped and turned to me. "Do you intend to go with Eleanor on the bus?"

I said, "Yes, I do."

He replied quickly, "You'll be the only white person on the bus. We don't know what will happen; it could be very dangerous. Are you sure you want to do this?"

Wide-eyed and miffed, I stood straighter as I said, "If Eleanor's going, then I'm going." But I was thinking, *Man, does this guy think I'm afraid of those lily-livered bullies?*

With a skeptical attitude, he took our names, addresses, and phone numbers. I didn't see or hear from him again until three months later, when he contacted me about the bus ride. Then, on the day we were to load the buses, there he was with the black leaders, helping wherever needed. As soon as Syrus saw us, he came over to say hello and told us which bus line to stand in. He gave us some quick instructions and then disappeared back into the crowd.

Rachel went back in time, visualizing every detail of the days that followed. She wasn't sure what she was telling the doctor, because her vivid recollection took over her memory and her mouth.

She heard herself describing the scene: "A huge crowd had gathered to watch. And, of course, the KKK was there in their white robes and their leering ugliness. When the buses finally arrived, we formed a line to get on. I felt a chill go up my spine as the crowd parted and a KKK member walked straight toward me. He growled, 'Hey, little lady' and, with an obnoxious grin, raised a shotgun from under his robe and aimed it right into my face. I froze, my heart fell to my feet, and all I could think was, *He's wearing a huge cross around his neck, and he's going to kill me because I won't allow him to think for me.* He leaned in close enough for me to smell alcohol on his breath as he said, 'You get on that bus, and we'll track you down and hang you from the tree in front of your Ma and Pa's house.'

"I couldn't speak, I couldn't move, and my head was swimming as though I would pass out. From out of nowhere, an arm caught me at the waist and pulled me to safety. It was Syrus, and he had a police officer in tow with him. That cop was real nice when he talked to the lowlife KKK scum and his cronies while asking them to kindly move back. However, that same cop did not say a word to me, although Syrus asked if I was okay. I was shaking like a leaf, but I said I was fine. He could see I really wasn't, so he pulled me in close to him and held me tight.

"Then he softly said, "You should go back home; this is just the beginning, and it's going to get worse. If anything happened to you, I would feel responsible."

"Feeling lucid again, I pushed back away from him, stood my ground, and boldly announced, 'Nothing is going to happen to me; I'm going.'

"Frankly, I was more determined than ever to get on that bus after what had just happened. Something snapped in me. I felt a whole new meaning to life. I did have a brain, I could think for myself, and I was going to stand up for what I believed in.

"And as sure as I felt about going, I also felt relieved when the buses pulled out of Memphis. Everyone on the bus was nice, and some said I was their hero. I didn't feel like a hero, and I didn't feel like I was in any danger once we left Memphis.

"But that day's emotional intensity was certainly matched by the

blazing sun and extreme humidity. And even though the windows were open, and we all had fans, it was miserable on that bus. Sy was driving a car and in charge of getting food and cold drinks whenever we came into a not-so-friendly town, which was every town we entered. Sidney Blumberg, Sy's fraternity brother, rode with him. Our first stop was outside of Nashville. We drove into the woods and stopped in a shantytown with lots of shade trees. And believe me, we were all happy to get off those buses for a while. Eleanor and I joined the meeting of group leaders to see if there was anything we could do to help. Milton, the main black leader for our drive to the state capital, announced their next stop would be outside of Knoxville, where they could get gas and food and we could all rest for a while before driving all night. Everyone agreed. Sy said that would give him and Sidney time to get food and drinks for everybody. I quickly volunteered to go into town with them, announcing that after all, three could get more than two. They both smiled and agreed that I could be of help.

"Later, when we arrived outside of Knoxville—the hometown of UT, our college—I got into the car with them, and we drove into town. The boys wanted to go to their favorite watering hole and have a cold beer. I ordered iced tea. Once we ordered our drinks, Sy smiled at me and asked, 'How are you doing?'

"'I'm fine. Everyone is very nice to me, but it's hot as blazes on that bus.'

"Sy looked directly into my eyes, smiling as he remarked, 'It's really brave of you to do this. I never even considered that a southern white girl would do such a dangerous thing.'

"'Well, as my Grandma Zola always said, it's no hill for a climber.'

"'You're a courageous climber! Here's what I think we should do. Sidney, you go to the grocery store and get what they have on the list. I can go to Ma Brown's Chicken Shack and buy as much fried chicken as I can without them asking too many questions, and then, Rachel, maybe you could go into the other restaurant and order more chicken to go.' My mind was going ninety to nothing trying to figure out a way that Sy and I could go together. Then it hit me, so I set down my glass and with a grin said, 'Hey, I have an idea. Why don't you and I go into Ma Brown's together all googly-eyed and holding hands and tell them we need to order lots of chicken to take to my family reunion over in Johnson City. We could order fifty or sixty pieces, and I bet they wouldn't say a thing, because you know how everybody thinks young lovers are a little goofy anyway. It will take a while for them to get that much chicken ready, so then we could go to the next restaurant and do the same thing. We could get out of town before anyone compares notes.' Sidney and Syrus looked at each other and said simultaneously, 'Good idea.'

"We finished our drinks and trekked less than three blocks to Ma Brown's. I was already so crazy about Sy. My heart was racing as I took his hand, hoping he wouldn't give me a weird look, but he just smiled and winked at me as he squeezed my hand. I had never been in love before, and I was amazed at my own reaction. I was so deliriously happy. I could not stop smiling, and I remember thinking, 'It won't be hard to pretend to be lovers.'

"When we placed the order, no one seemed concerned. They just said it would take an hour, and Syrus said that was fine and we'd be back in an hour. At the next restaurant, we decided to sit down and eat while we waited for the order. Again no one seemed concerned about us, but we could overhear conversations of them talking about the buses out on Highway 40 and how they had better not come into their town. Syrus and I just smiled at each other as I talked about how exciting it was that he was going to meet my family and how they would love him. The patrons, suspicious of all strangers, were listening to every word we said, so I threw in 'Lord Jesus' every so often just to fit in. After all, I was from Memphis and Sy was from Oxford, Mississippi, so it wasn't a stretch. We had fun with our role-playing as a couple. He called me 'sweetie' and pulled me in close to him and I called him 'honey' and took the opportunity to hug and touch him all I could, without being too obvious. At the time, I was sure that he enjoyed it as much as I did; but when we returned to the buses, he became distant toward me, and I began to wonder if it hadn't just been my wishful thinking.

"But I felt really good about us getting all that chicken. Everyone joined in for a wonderful picnic under the stars with plenty of food, cold drinks, and ice. Sidney had bought bags and bags of ice. Everyone grabbed hands full and rubbed it all over their bodies. It was like manna from heaven in that heat. Later that evening, we all were excited to get back on the buses and get to Washington, DC. Every time we stopped for gas and food, I helped Sidney and Syrus get what we needed, but we were never together again like we were in Knoxville."

Dr. Schaffer, intrigued, leaned in and asked, "Then what happened?"

"Once we got to Washington, I spent most of my time with Syrus and Marty. I was so glad I had taken the risk to be a part of such a momentous event. The energy in the air was joyous and hopeful. I felt no danger from anyone and was surprised to see a lot of white people were there.

"Martin Luther King Jr. was mesmerizing; it seemed as if he were speaking words channeled from God. It became crystal-clear to me that all the black people were asking for was to be respected and accepted—the same thing every human being wanted. I was ashamed of the South and what we had done to our own black people. I had never felt it as clearly as I did on that day. I remember wondering if I would have been as aware if I had missed that auspicious event. It changed me in ways I cannot even explain. That tangible sadness that I had seen in my European Jewish grandparents' eyes I could see in the eyes of the black people all around me. I knew that my grandparents had been treated horribly in Europe. They had not been accepted and were looked down on, cursed, beaten, and killed for no reason except their religion. The churches had done a good job of teaching hatred toward the Jews, and the Jews paid a price for their loyalty to God. Syrus and I talked about it at length. His family had their own stories of degradation and loss. We talked about how, in some ways, the Jews' past compared to the current situation. We had both heard about the hatred and cruel prejudice directed toward the Jews in Europe, and we had seen that same prejudice directed toward black people in our own hometowns. We were so glad we had come to hear Martin Luther King Jr. It made a profound difference in how we looked at the civil rights issue. It was something that changed us and would stay with us for the rest of our lives."

a strong connection for so long, but somewhere along the way we lost that special bond we had between us. Both of us worked so much, and the kids took a lot of my time. In all fairness, I really didn't notice the distance between us until both kids left for college. But I did notice we'd both changed. It was like we were on two different islands and neither one of us wanted to dive in and swim to the other's island."

Dr. Schaffer was stroking his beard while nodding. "Yes, I see. However, from what I heard from Syrus, I don't believe he wants a divorce. But he is obviously not hearing what you need. I have an idea of something I would like you to try. It's called a date night. This is a time when you set aside a specific time to go to dinner—not a movie or party, but someplace where you can talk. You do have an issue with communication. Try to find out information on a case he's trying, from his secretary or possibly the newspaper, and then ask a probing question about the case. Focus on him and only him, not the kids or household issues; bring up something that would appeal to his vanity. See if you can get him into an in-depth conversation.

"I wouldn't worry about sex right now. I know several men who are taking those meds and having the same problem. He will have to try different medications until they find one that works for him. He needs to stay on the drugs. He is in a high-stress job, and you don't want him to have a heart attack. Hopefully you can get him to go on that vacation, which would help his stress level more than anything else, probably. In the meantime, try to plan a specific date night every week and let me know how that works out. I'm also going to give you a prescription for Valium. You told me over the phone you were having problems sleeping and eating. The anxiety you are going through with the loss of your sister, who was also your closest friend, coupled with your marriage issues would cause any person a high level of anxiety. I'm going to give you fifteen pills to start with. Don't take them during the day. Take them only at night. A good night's sleep could help you. Then check back in with me in a week to tell me how you are doing, and let's set another appointment for two weeks from today."

"A good night's sleep would be a welcome change." As Rachel got up to leave, she smiled and said, "Thank you, Doctor."

14

RACHEL WENT HOME INSTEAD OF GOING BACK TO THE OFFICE. SHE made some tea while going over in her mind the meeting with Dr. Schaffer. She had made an appointment to see him again. There was so much more she needed to tell him. She wanted his opinion on her feelings about Hope's death—how she thought Sammy and Alfie were hiding something from her about Hope's death. She wanted to tell him about the sequence of events leading up to her death. She wanted to know whether he could give her insight into why she couldn't let it go. Something about the story bothered her, and she wondered whether it was all in her head, as Sy insinuated.

That morning she had stopped by an expensive men's clothing store to pick up some dress shirts for Sy and was surprised to see Alfred and Sammy shopping. Alfred was trying on a cashmere sports coat, and Sammy was telling him how great he looked. Sammy was so happy, as if he had forgotten Hope had died. Rachel put on her best pasted-on smile and went over to greet them. She approached them and said, "Alfred, that fits you perfectly and looks great."

Mumbling, he said, "Thank you," but he would not look her in the eyes.

Sammy lunged, grabbing her for an endearing embrace. "My dear, sweet sister-in-law, I've been meaning to call you, but it's still so hard to talk about my beloved Hope." Tears formed as he slumped and looked at her with a hangdog expression. "I miss my darling Hope so much. I'm sure you feel the same. I'm sorry I haven't reached out to you. It's taking all my energy to get through the day. We must get together soon." His effusive emotional display was phony and overdone. His actions seemed strange to Rachel, because he had never acted so distraught before, not even when their baby boy died from crib death two months after Diane's second birthday. Although Rachel couldn't bring herself to believe that Sammy had anything to do with Hope's death, she also could not understand Sammy and Alfred's weird behavior. It made her wonder if Sammy was covering up for Alfred, for something he had done. She could not let go of the feeling that they were hiding something from her.

As she poured the hot water into her teacup, Rachel heard the piano in the den playing and thought Mindy must be home, but she then remembered her daughter had already gone back to college. Curious, she went into the den to see what the sound was. Maybe the stereo was on. As she looked around, she noticed the piano's keyboard cover was up and the picture of her and Hope had been moved. A strong smell of perfume permeated the area next to the piano. She recognized the smell; it was Norell, the perfume Hope always wore. The stereo was not on, and there was no sound of any kind. She felt shaky, drawing herself away from the piano as she slowly backed out of the room. When she returned to the kitchen, she realized she was shaking and crying. What had just happened? Was she losing her grip on reality? She sat down at the kitchen table and tried to calm herself, praying for strength, for fear she was having a mental breakdown.

Outside, roaring winds and quaking thunder had quickly moved in. Followed by a torrential downpour, with rain pounding so hard on the roof and windows that the echo reverberating throughout the house sounded as though someone was beating on the doors and windows, demanding to be let inside, exacerbating Rachel's dark mood. She could not stop shaking; she was so confused and weary. She could not make sense of anything, and all she wanted to do now was take a Valium and go to sleep. She called Sy's office, but he didn't answer his phone, so she silently prayed he was on his way home; she did not want to be alone. She picked up her cup of tea, went upstairs, and curled up in the built-in window seat in their bedroom. As she stared out the window through the bleakness of her soul, she felt as if the lightning were striking out at her, and she wondered what she had ever done to merit God's scorn. Her life had become a nightmare she could not change or escape. If only she could wake up and have everything be the same as it had been three months before, she'd change her ways, she would keep the Sabbath, and she'd spend more time helping others.

She was jolted from her stupor when the bedroom door unexpectedly opened and Sy walked in. He took one look at her and stopped. "What's wrong with you? You look peaked."

She tried not to cry, but she couldn't stop herself. Her hands were trembling so much that she had to set her teacup down. "I feel like I'm losing my mind. I know there is something wrong with how Hope died—something they are not telling me. You're going to think I'm crazy too, but I swear to you Hope was here today … Or her ghost was anyway."

Sy tugged at his tie and unbuttoned his shirt collar, contemplating what she had said. "What do you mean, 'her ghost'?"

"I know this sounds strange, please don't make fun of me, but I swear I heard the piano playing, so I went into the den and saw the piano lid was up. The picture of me and Hope had been moved, and I could smell her perfume."

"Oh honey, Mindy probably left the lid up. You just wish she was here so much that your mind is playing tricks on you."

"I don't think so. A picture of Hope and Sammy fell right in front of me at their house within an hour after the funeral, and now a picture has been moved on the piano; it's too much of a coincidence."

Sy walked over, knelt down next to her, and took her hand. "Rachel, I miss her too, and I wish there were something I could do, but ultimately, you're going to have to accept that she's gone."

"I know, I know, honey." Rachel turned to him and hugged him tightly. "I'm so glad you're home; let's go out to dinner tonight, okay?"

"Sure. Are you ready?"

"Let me freshen up my makeup; it'll just take a minute."

As she went into the bathroom, she called out to him, "What are you doing home so early?"

"I had a run-in with one of my old criminal clients today. I despise the man, and I didn't feel that I could properly represent him. I tried to hand him off to one of the other attorneys in the office, but he went ballistic. He would not leave my office, so I left. I had all I could take. I'm afraid he's the type who would try to shoot me because I won't do what he wants. He really needs to be in a mental institution; however, the laws don't give that option until he kills someone. That's a law that really needs to be challenged, but that would take an act of congress."

"I left so he'd have time to cool down. I called Alex after I left and told him to tell the guy to leave or they would call the police. I also told Alex we need to start locking the front and back doors and have the receptionist make visitors identify themselves and who they are there to see. And tomorrow I'm going to file a restraining order."

Rachel said, "Good," and she came out of the bathroom smiling, pleased that he was giving her more than a two-word answer.

As Sy and Rachel walked to the car, Sy said, "There's something I need to discuss with you before I make a decision."

"What is it?"

"Let's get to the restaurant, and then we'll talk about it."

Sy called the restaurant, Folks Folly, on his car phone. He requested one of their private rooms. He did not want anyone listening in on his conversation. Once they were seated and had their drinks, he floundered in his attempt to explain his dilemma as he drank his vodka on the rocks.

"What is it?" Rachel asked, a worried crease to her brow. "You're worrying me."

He ordered another drink before continuing. "I'm considering leaving my law practice to run for a judgeship. It will cost a lot of money. It will also mean a big drop in my income. I think we would have to sell the house. The upkeep on the pool, the yard, and the house is huge. I'd like to move to a zero-lot line house with very little maintenance. I do want to go on vacations, but most of all I want to have more time with you and the kids. I do not want a divorce. I need your support to do this. It means a better life for us but with a lot less money. How do you feel about it?"

Rachel sat back, eyebrows lifted, and said, "Well, that would be fine with me. I've been worried about the constant stress you're under. You are working excessively. You need to slow down or you won't live long enough to enjoy your retirement. So what would happen if you lose?"

"I would continue in my law practice and consider my options. I could run again for a judgeship or run for the state attorney general."

"Okay, I'd be happy to move into a zero-lot line house. In the meantime, let's get out of town for a week or two when the courts close in December. Let's go to the Caribbean and lie out on the beach and veg out."

"I can't go for more than five days. But yes, let's leave on Friday morning and come back on a Wednesday. I really need a few days in my office to catch up on my backlog of work while the courts are closed."

Laughing, she said, "Okay, I'll take that. Let's go back to the Cayman Islands resort where we stayed ten years ago."

"Sure. It's close enough it won't take all day to get there. Maybe we could leave on Thursday afternoon."

"Great. I'll check on flights first thing tomorrow.

Their waiter brought in Sy's drink, took their dinner order, and, like a ninja warrior, left so swiftly Rachel was not sure he had been there at all.

Sy and Rachel continued talking and joking about the possibilities, both relieved of their own anxieties. When they got home, they went to bed, turned on the TV, and cuddled, falling asleep in each other's arms. For the first time since Hope's death, Rachel slept through the night without a Valium and woke up invigorated.

misses you so much. I'm also hearing something about a boat; does that mean anything to you?"

Rachel quickly whispered, "Yes, but I really can't talk about this here. Can I make an appointment with you? Do you think she will come back if we have a private reading?"

"I can't guarantee it, but usually the spirit will come back if it has more to say, and I feel like she needs to talk with you. Would you like my card?"

"Yes." Rachel took her card as she heard herself say, "I've been through a really rough time lately. I'd like to see you as soon as possible. When could you meet with me?"

After checking schedules, they settled on Thursday afternoon.

"The address is on my card."

Rachel looked down at the card. "I'll be there. Thank you so much, Mrs. Evans."

Rachel watched as the woman pulled out of the parking lot and wondered if she should keep the appointment. She had not been to a psychic before and began to question her own sanity. She thought maybe she should call Dr. Schaffer instead.

By the following Thursday, all apprehension had dissipated and she was counting the hours before she could leave to meet with the psychic.

As Rachel pulled up in front of Darlene Evans's house, she couldn't help but notice how it stood out from the other houses on the street. It was a quaint cottage-style white house with black trim and roof, a white picket fence and a white stone walkway. Stone arches stood between white Doric columns on the front porch.

As she walked up to the door, she saw Darlene standing in the doorway to welcome her. She led Rachel through the living room and down a hallway to a cozy room with a fireplace flanked by bookshelves. On the opposite wall stood an altar under a large portrait of a bushy-haired man in an orange gown standing with his hands facing up and forward, as if he were blessing them. Candles flickered around him and incense filled the room with a pleasant aroma. The walls and furniture were in subtle shades of green and beige. Darlene directed Rachel to an overstuffed chair and told her to meditate on what she wanted to ask about while Darlene went to get some iced tea for them. The energy in the room was warm and inviting, and Rachel felt completely at ease.

While Darlene was getting situated in the chair across from her, Rachel inquired, "Who's the man in the picture?"

Darlene looked up intently, smiling at the picture. "That's my guru, Sai Baba. He's a holy man from India. I could talk about him for hours, but right now we need to focus on you. Have you brought me an item from your loved one?"

Nodding, Rachel handed her Hope's antique ring. "I'm so grateful you could see me on such short notice. My sister died in June, and ever since then I've been a mess; I can't sleep … I can't eat." Rachel pointed at the ring and said, "That's a ring she had on her finger the day she died."

"Yes, I'm hearing the old gospel song 'Faith, Hope, and Charity.'"

"Her name is Hope, and she was the epitome of all three—the kindest, most loving woman you would ever want to know."

"Yes, I can feel her presence here. She is a beautiful soul. Have you ever had someone from the other side channeled for you?"

"Oh no, I've never done anything like this before. Playing with an eight ball is as close as I've ever come to anything psychic."

Darlene laughed. "Well, this is a little bit different. I need to tell you I have no control over who comes in, but they will come in to validate what you need to help you. Your loved ones are always with you in spirit."

Rachel nodded vigorously and said, "I do need to know my sister is okay."

"Yes. I'm going to go into a meditation to connect to the spirits of loved ones who have crossed over."

"Okay." Rachel closed her eyes as she took deep breaths and waited anxiously, not knowing what to expect.

Darlene embraced the ring as she closed her eyes and mumbled to herself. She sat there for a few minutes before raising her head, and then, eyes still closed, she said, "Yes, Hope is so happy you're here."

Rachel's eyes popped open, and she began to sob as she cried out, "Hope, I'm so lost without you."

Darlene abruptly stopped and opened her eyes. She touched Rachel's hand and gently spoke. "Rachel, you've got to remain calm and loving. I cannot channel if you are in extreme anguish and pain. It causes trauma for me, and I cannot continue. Can you stay calm and quiet and let Hope come through and talk?"

Rachel stopped short and took a deep breath. "I'm so sorry. I can … I will. I do want to hear from her more than anything in the world. I'll calm down."

"Try to remember happy times—times when you felt good and grateful. Nothing negative. Please give me a minute to get back into trance, and then ask to speak to her; but you must come from love, not anguish, okay?"

Rachel wiped away her tears and took deep breaths. "Yes, yes, I will. I swear I will." Rachel closed her eyes, thinking, *Hope, I love you so much. I've been so blessed to have you in my life. I need to talk to you.*

Suddenly Hope started talking through Darlene. "I love you too. I miss you all so much. It wasn't my time to go."

Rachel opened her eyes halfway; she was amazed at how the psychic had the same mannerisms and the same way of speaking as Hope.

Rachel softly said, "Hope, we miss you too. What do you mean it wasn't your time to go?"

pressure already with the workload I have; I don't need any more wild goose chases to go on."

Rachel stood defiant. "I thought marriage was about supporting each other through thick and thin."

"I support you extremely well."

"Emotionally … things are always on your terms. You keep making decisions for us without considering my feelings. What about what I want?"

Sy looked up at her. He wanted to get up, but she had him blocked in. "What about this house? Your car?"

Rachel said emphatically, "I bought my own car. And I have a successful business too, in case you hadn't noticed." She flailed her arms in the air. "But why would you notice? You never notice anything!"

Sy spoke softly, hoping to calm her. "Honey, I know you have always contributed your fair share, but I feel you need to think about what you're asking. Maybe talk this over with your therapist before we contemplate doing something so extreme."

"Well, I don't. The problem is I should have spoken up a long time ago, instead of saying nothing and just letting things go. That was my mistake!"

"What's that supposed to mean?"

"I ask you to do one teeny, tiny little thing that would only take a phone call, and that's asking too much. I used to believe I knew you, but now I feel like I'm married to a stranger. So let me put it in terms you can relate to." Frustrated, she slammed her fist on the end table. "I want you out of this house until we can decide if this sham of a marriage is worth saving."

"You're throwing me out of the house because I don't want to take the word of a psychic?"

"No, that's just the tip of the iceberg. You don't take anything I say as valid, and I'm tired of being ignored. I'll put your things in the guest house until you can find a place." She stormed out of the den, muttering under her breath. Enraged she ran up the stairs to their bedroom closet and started throwing his clothes into a laundry basket. Then she walked back down to the den and dropped the basket at his feet.

Sy just sat there shaking his head, chin thrust out with his black eyes piercing through her, which made her even more furious. She turned her back on him, biting her tongue to keep from screaming. Instead she went upstairs, slammed the bedroom door, and locked it.

Syrus worried about Rachel. She was changing before his eyes. She had been complaining for months about their marriage, even insisting on seeing a family therapist, and maybe he had pushed her away. Their sex life was slim to none because of his high blood pressure and those damn pills he had to take, plus he was exhausted most of the time. He had backed himself into a corner by taking on too many cases. He needed more help with his cases, more research assistance; but like his father, he could not ask for help. His family considered it a weakness to ask for help. Practicing law took a tremendous amount of mental dedication, and he was starting to forget little things. He had to become much more disciplined in his work habits for fear of making a costly mistake. When he was younger, he could remember everything, but now he needed to write it all down. He was not prepared for how aging was taking a toll on him.

Was Rachel really going to leave him? He couldn't believe she had gone to the extreme of kicking him out of the house, even though it was just a few steps out the back door to the guest house. He began to consider, for the first time, she might be serious about divorce. She was right about checking on the insurance policy; it would be an easy thing for him to do.

Their marriage had been good for so long; maybe he did take it for granted. He knew he had become a workaholic, but it seemed to him he had no choice. Their marriage had changed so slowly, and he hadn't realized it was changing until it was too late. But how could he change it back? He was focused on his cases most of the time. They had a busy social life, and he was with her every weekend. He felt as though everything was piling up on him. How much more did he have to give?

17

Sʏ ᴡᴏᴋᴇ ᴜᴘ ᴛʜᴇ ɴᴇxᴛ ᴍᴏʀɴɪɴɢ ᴄᴏɴꜰᴜsᴇᴅ ᴀs ʜᴇ ʟᴏᴏᴋᴇᴅ ᴀʀᴏᴜɴᴅ the strange room and then remembered the fight. He wanted a cup of coffee but did not want to go into the house and have to deal with Rachel. He would give her time to cool down. He quickly dressed and left for his office, where there was always coffee ready.

As he was driving, he kept going over the argument with Rachel in his mind. He knew she was despondent and having a rough time dealing with her sister's death, but he did not realize how bad it had become. He didn't know what he could do to help, but he did not think encouraging this psychic thing was the right approach. He had so much on his plate, including a big trial starting on Monday that he would have to prepare for all weekend. Maybe he should ask Sara to take Rachel to a grief support group. Sara would listen to him, and he was sure she would try to help; it would be helpful for her as well. He could have the life insurance checked on too. He was sure there would be *some* life insurance, but if there was not a million-dollar policy, then he could prove to Rachel the psychic was bogus, and that would be the end of it. He felt he had found the solution and started thinking about whom to contact to verify the information.

As soon as he arrived at his office, he called the detective agency that he often used when necessary. He asked to speak with Josh Myers. "Hi Josh, Syrus Marcus. I need you to look into something for me."

"Sure, Sy, what can I help you with?"

"I have a client that suspects there is a life insurance policy missing from an estate; I am handling it as a favor for a friend. I need you to track down the insurance policies on the deceased. I need to find all life insurance policies, especially anything over a hundred thousand dollars, that have been taken out on her. I know the insurance agent they always used, because I use him too. But listen; I do not want you to disclose this information to anyone. It is a personal matter. The deceased is Hope Grossman. I'm sending over an envelope with her Social Security number, address, date of death, and all the other pertinent information you will need. As well as the insurance agent's information. Also, I'd like to have your findings as soon as possible."

"Okay, I'll get right on it. I'll call you as soon as I have all the information."

"Thanks, Josh."

Syrus put his hands around his face and rubbed his temples. His head was throbbing, and he felt he was on the verge of crying. He decided to wait to call his mother-in-law until he got the results from the detective. If there was no million-dollar policy, it would be easier to convince Rachel she needed help.

18

RACHEL HAD TOSSED AND TURNED ALL NIGHT. SHE FINALLY GAVE UP on trying to sleep and went to the kitchen to make coffee. As she measured the coffee, she stopped for a minute, realizing she needed to make enough for only one person. Instead of crying, a flood of emotion came over her as her jaw tightened and her cheeks flushed with leftover anger at Sy. She reflected on how he'd said, "What's important to you is important to me." That was just a lie. It was a way to keep her in her place—a way to shut her up. He underestimated her. He wanted some hard evidence, and she was going to find some. She still had the key to Hope and Sammy's house, and she knew the house was up for sale, with most of the furniture still in it. She also knew the real estate agent handling the sale was Sharon Chambliss, Hope's friend who was on the yacht when she died.

Sharon was another person of interest, because Rachel's friend Jennifer had stopped in her shop to tell her that Sammy had been seen out at dinner with Sharon. Jennifer told her that other people were also talking about it and that she was wondering whether Rachel knew anything about them dating, because it appeared they had been leaning close to each other, talking and acting somewhat intimate. Rachel was surprised by the gossip, and her mind was reeling from the sudden insight that Sammy had probably been having an affair with her before Hope died.

Rachel hurriedly dressed and poured her coffee into a travel cup and headed for her showroom. She called Sharon as soon as she arrived. Sharon didn't answer, so Rachel left a message asking her to please return her call. She wanted to ask not only about the sale of the house but also about how poor Sammy was faring since the loss of his beloved wife. She was dying to hear Sharon's explanation.

Rachel was going to take the investigation into her own hands. She was sure there were many personal items left in the house, because Diane had been complaining about all the things Sammy was asking her to do to help empty the house. However, Diane was still working full-time and had told Rachel she was going to do it after she left on her maternity leave.

After hanging up the phone, she went into the showroom to determine where she could place a mannequin to display her latest creation—a satin-and-lace ball gown. She looked around, remembering the excitement of opening day for her dress shop, Designs for the Times of Your Life! Rachel had decorated her shop ethereally, with billowy chiffon and silk fabrics festooned around the room, pinned in place with drawings of her creations. She had gone to estate sales and antique stores in Mississippi, Arkansas, and Louisiana, looking for antique furniture, dress forms, and vintage gowns, as well as vintage satin, taffeta, and lace. She had purchased an antique armoire for the display of tiaras, jewelry, ring-bearer pillows, and angel gift items. Rachel had a surround sound system installed to play celestial music in the background and had strategically placed scented candles around the showroom that she would light before opening. She wanted her shop to feel as close to heaven as possible. Rachel had loved every minute of it and was anxious to build a queendom where women could have gowns custom made to suit their style and taste to celebrate the most joyous occasion of their lives. On one side of the floor-to-ceiling windows facing the street, she had displayed a white satin wedding gown with a rhinestone-dotted belt, a tulle skirt, and illusion sleeves. On the other side of the ornate entry doors, an off-the-shoulder floral lace over a cerulean silk ball gown was on display.

She was happy for the first time since Hope's death, knowing there was something she could do to help her sister. She grabbed the phone when it rang; she could see on her caller ID that it was Sharon. "Hi, Sharon."

Sharon sounded surprised as she answered. "Hi, Rachel, it's so nice to hear from you. How are you doing?"

"I'm muddling through. I miss Hope so much. I was hoping we could go to lunch or dinner soon. I know Hope considered you a good friend. I need someone I can talk to about her; would you indulge me?"

"Of course; I miss her too. When do you want to meet?"

"Would Thursday, either lunch or dinner, work for you?"

"Yes, dinner would be best. I rarely show a house after six o'clock."

"Great. So, I saw you have Hope and Sammy's house listed; how is that going? Are there any serious buyers yet?"

"No, it's an expensive house, and in Memphis there is a small market for a million-dollar home. In addition, most buyers spending that much money want to move out east in the River Oaks or Germantown neighborhoods. It takes a certain kind of person to purchase a historical house. So where would you like to meet for dinner?"

They agreed to meet at Grisanti's restaurant at six thirty on Thursday night.

Rachel was jazzed. She started calculating when a good time would be to sneak into Hope and Sammy's house. Probably before 9:00 a.m. on Thursday; that would give her time to get back to her shop by ten thirty. She needed to call Sammy's office to see whether he was out of town. She remembered Diane telling her Sammy and Alfie were going on a business trip. She wanted to make sure he would not be stopping by the house on Thursday. She dialed the number and asked to speak to Alfie.

"I'm sorry; Alfie and Sammy are out of town on a business trip. Do you want to leave a message?"

"No. When will they be back in the office?"

"Not until next Monday."

"Okay, thanks."

was going to make him send Alfie home so they could have their time together."

Rachel and Sharon finished their meal and said their goodbyes, both saying they should get together again. However, Rachel suspected neither was sincere about meeting again. And if Sharon were having an affair with Sammy, she would lie about it to everyone, especially to her. We tell so many red and white lies; the little white lies we tell other people and the big ones we tell ourselves.

SYRUS WAS THINKING IT HAD BEEN OVER TWO WEEKS SINCE HE HAD talked to Josh Myers when his phone rang.

"Hi, Sy; Josh Myers."

"Hi, Josh. You have some information for me?"

"Yes, I do. I've not only found important information for you but also some documents you're going to want to see. Can you meet with me today, around five o'clock?"

"Make it closer to five thirty, if you don't mind."

"Sure. See you then."

Sy was apprehensive as he waited for Josh to arrive. His office window air conditioner was running, but he was sweating. As he got out of his chair to go lower the thermostat, there was a knock on his door.

"Come in!"

The young detective came in and thrust his hand forward, giving Sy a firm handshake. Sy waved him to a chair and continued to the air conditioner. Before Sy could get back to his chair, Josh started telling him about his findings.

"There were three different life insurance policies: one for twenty-five thousand and one for two hundred thousand, taken out fifteen

20

AFTER MEETING WITH THE FBI, SY ASCERTAINED THAT HE COULD HAVE jurisdiction in Tennessee, pursuant to what port the body had been brought back through. He guessed Florida would most likely have been the port of entry. If it was, he would have to research Florida's law pertaining to jurisdiction. He started thinking through all the different steps it would take to find out Hope's cause of death. He called in his new law clerk to do the research on what port the body had been brought into. If, and it was a big if, they could try the case in Tennessee, the next order of business would be to get an order to exhume the body for an autopsy. To do that, Sy would have to get the district attorney to work with him to get the order. He was not going to mention it to Rachel until he got all the facts. He didn't want to get her hopes up and then disappoint her. Besides, he was still in the doghouse (i.e., the guesthouse) so he didn't see her much; and half the time, she wouldn't take his calls. There was really nothing to tell her until he knew if it could be tried in Tennessee. And he didn't want her badgering him to take it to court when it wasn't up to him. That would be the DA's call, and he was going to want hard evidence and facts to substantiate that a crime had been committed.

He called Bryan Ramsey, the first black attorney to be elected to the DA's office in Memphis. Bryan was a brilliant prosecutor who had a reputation for doing the important and difficult cases himself. Sy liked him from the first time he met him. He believed Bryan was destined to be a successful attorney as well as a politician. Sy was also one of the few lawyers who believed Bryan could win, and he never forgot that Syrus had called him on the eve of the election to wish him good luck. Most of the white lawyers were backing his opponent, and they were surprised and disgruntled when he did win.

"Bryan, Sy Marcus here. I have a real dilemma on a case. I need to discuss my options with you. Any chance you could meet me for a game of golf on Saturday?"

"This coming Saturday?"

"Yes."

"Okay, where and what time?"

Joking, Sy said, "Do you know where the 'Jews Are Us' country club in Germantown is, off Poplar?" Laughing heartily, he added, "How about eight in the morning? If we go much later, it'll be as hot as Hades."

They agreed upon eight thirty.

Syrus waited anxiously for Saturday morning's golf game, going over the different scenarios in his head of how to ask Ramsey about getting an exhumation order, should he need it. Since there was a million-dollar policy, he was now going to have to go to the extreme of determining the cause of death to satisfy Rachel and, he hoped, give her the closure she needed. Then, in the unlikely event something should come of the results of the autopsy, he would have to come up with evidence to convince Ramsey to take the case to court.

They walked the golf course, talking between shots. Sy wanted to keep the conversation light, so he casually told jokes while managing to fill Bryan in on the circumstances surrounding Hope's death, as well as giving him the information he had researched on the jurisdiction issue. Sy had just finished his favorite lawyer joke when Bryan said, "I've got a good one for you," and launched into his joke, getting to the punch line.

"So the attorney says, 'St. Peter, I don't get it. The pope devoted his whole life to serving God, and his final resting place looks like a room at Motel 6. I'm just an attorney, and my quarters look like Buckingham Palace. Why?' St. Peter replies, 'Look, we're up to our asses in popes up here ... You're the first attorney that has ever made it!'

Sy burst out laughing as they stopped to tee up for their next shot. After both men hit great shots, they had a long walk to the next hole. Sy continued in a voice both subdued and perplexed. "Ramsey, I know it sounds odd, but I do give credence to women's intuition. Whenever my wife has expressed something that she says she knew instinctively, she has usually been right."

"Yeah, so other than your wife's intuition, do you have any facts to substantiate a possible murder?"

"The victim's husband received over a million dollars in assets, plus he collected on a million-dollar life insurance policy that was barely two years old, and it was paid without an autopsy. Under the circumstances, that is unusual, to say the least."

"Yes, that's a solid motive—but not enough to prosecute."

"Yes, but my wife is obsessed with this; she's threatening to leave me if I don't help her. I'm going to have to dig deeper, get an autopsy done to make sure it wasn't a murder ... so I can sleep at night ... in my own bed." Both men laughed knowingly.

After the golf game, Sy drove to his office going over all the details of Hope's death. The hardest thing for him to wrap his head around was that Sammy might be gay. He couldn't see it; Sammy had a reputation of being a philanderer with women. That was the worst that he had heard about Sammy, and he had known him most of his life. He had always gotten along with his brother-in-law. He treated Hope well, except for the philandering, which Hope either didn't know about or chose to ignore. Sy also could not believe Sammy was a murderer; he just wasn't the type. Could Alfred have murdered her? And if so, how did he get it past the coroner? Had he planned it ahead of time and bought off the coroner? But how would he know what port they would go into? Moreover, if Sammy wasn't gay, what could explain the weird relationship Sammy had with Alfred? None of it made sense.

21

SAMMY PULLED INTO THE PARKING LOT OF MEDNIKOW JEWELERS, THE same place he had purchased Hope's diamond ring. He greeted the owner, Maurice, with a smile and handed him Hope's wedding ring with the three-carat round diamond.

"Maurice, I'd like to have this diamond put into a new setting for me. Could you give me an idea of what you can do with it?"

"Certainly, Mr. Grossman; I have a number of settings you can choose from. Let's go into my private office, where I can bring in several things for you to look at. Can I get you some coffee or something to drink?"

"Yes. You don't happen to have some of that scotch I imported for you, do you?"

"I sure do." He opened the door and motioned him to a cushy leather office chair next to a small, ornate conference table. He picked up a nearby phone and ordered a scotch on the rocks for Sammy.

Sammy was flush with delight as he pondered all the choices for a ring for himself. After attempting to see the diamond next to the settings he had picked out, he turned to Maurice. "Can you take the

23

As Darlene Evans walked up the crumbling brick steps, she looked up at the ominous old southern mansion and an eerie feeling enveloped her. Images permeated the entire area as if she had been taken back to another era of history. Being a medium did have its drawbacks. She tried to force herself back into the twentieth century, to no avail.

Standing in a daze with the sun flickering through the leaves of the magnolia tree, she could hear a small child crying for help. It sounded as though it was coming from the balcony above. Darlene closed her eyes and shuddered, trying to throw off the feeling. She knew the cry was from a different century, a different world. She stood back and looked up at the house again. There was no balcony. She wondered why it was missing. She had read a little about this house in a Victorian Village brochure. She knew that it was pre–Civil War and that something had happened here during the occupation of Memphis. However, she wasn't here to delve into the secessionist history of the Civil War. Hers was a far more important and timely concern.

She turned the ornate brass knob to open the front door, but it did not budge. She looked up at the tall, narrow doors and couldn't help but wonder how the women in the nineteenth century could have gotten through them with a hoop skirt. As she leaned into the door, it suddenly gave way, and she lurched into the entry hall. Looking around, she admired the magnificent mahogany staircase that rose to the right. Down the center hallway, beautiful fluted woodwork with rosette moldings framed the double doors as well as the entry door. Directly in front of her was an unusual antique table. *It could be a Carlton House piece or a sofa table of sorts,* she thought. It seemed to be of Sheraton or Regency styling but was too ornate for either. She decided it was probably a handmade piece commissioned by one of the wealthy women of the plantation era. Darlene had loved antiques as far back as she could remember and, at one time, had seriously considered becoming an archeologist, but time and money had thwarted her ambitions.

Just as Darlene began to wonder if anyone was around, a young woman stepped out from a doorway in the far back of the house. Her voice echoed as she asked Darlene if she could help her.

"Yes, my name is Darlene Evans, and I have an appointment with Syrus Marcus."

The receptionist made her way to the desk and picked up the receiver; she dialed as she sat down. Annie's kind eyes looked up to Darlene, smiling as she talked. When she hung up the phone, she said, "Mr. Marcus is with someone right now but said to go on up the stairs to his seating area on the left and he'll be with you soon."

As soon as Darlene reached the top of the stairs, she saw a man standing shaking hands with another man. Syrus immediately turned to her and extended his hand to her. "Hello, I'm Syrus Marcus, and you must be Darlene Evans."

"Yes." As she reached out her hand to greet him, she felt as if he were an old friend. She smiled. "I'm very happy to meet you; I've heard wonderful things about you."

Smirking, he said, "Have you been talking to my press agent? Please come into my office. Can I get you iced tea or coffee?"

"Yes, iced tea would be great." She could feel a powerful energy emanating from him. He had a mystic coolness about him; he seemed emotionally controlled but mysterious, detached and self-possessed. He was of medium height with a husky build, strong shoulders, and muscular chest and arms, giving her the feeling, he could handle about anything. His playful eyes and pouty mouth gave him a youthful, mischievous look. If it weren't for his graying hair, she would have guessed him to be younger than he was. Darlene could see why Rachel was worried about losing him. He was most pleasing and had charisma galore.

Sy sat back behind his desk, smiling at her as he waited for her tea to be served. He was low key and charming as they talked. He began by asking about her work with the police department. After all the pleasantries, Syrus determined it was time to get down to business. "So how did you find out about the life insurance? I'm not trying to undermine you. I just need to know. In fact, I could pay you for inside information ... probably more than you're making as a psychic."

Darlene just smiled. "Aristotle said, 'It is the mark of an educated mind to be able to entertain a thought without accepting it.' Why don't you let me channel Hope so you can talk to her yourself?"

"So a ghost wants to retain me as her attorney? That's one for the books," Sy said with a wry grin. "You know, I've seen three psychics, and they all told me the same thing."

"Really? What was that?"

"'That'll be fifty dollars!'" Sy laughed gleefully at his own joke.

Darlene smiled; she could see how uncomfortable he was with the subject. She leaned in as she said, "Hope really needs your help ... She is in a lot of pain."

"How can she be in pain? She's dead."

"You know, just because someone murders you and you're dead does not mean you don't feel anything. You can only kill the body; you *cannot* kill the soul. The same way you can feel love, hatred, or hurt when you're alive is the same way you feel when your soul leaves your body. The soul interprets your emotions when you are in your body. The spirits have told me that the worst part after you're dead is that you can still feel the anguish and confusion, only you can now hear and feel others' emotions more openly."

"That's a sobering thought!"

"Yes, Hope can hear Sammy's thoughts and how happy he is to

have gotten rid of her. And it hurts her deeply, just as it would if she were alive."

"So why doesn't she just go to the light that you people claim is there?"

"Most people do … but she was in denial when she lived, and now she's in shock. She's confused and focused on what's happening here, and she needs our help to be able to let go of her anguish and go to the light."

Sy frowned as he tapped his fingers on the desk. "I don't know what I can do. She died in another country, not under United States jurisdiction, let alone the state of Tennessee. Besides, it would take a lot of my time—time I don't have. There is simply nothing I can do legally."

"I understand." Darlene smiled as she stood to leave, and she handed Syrus her card. Sy took the card and dropped it in his top left hand drawer. He remained seated as she left. He smiled and said, "I'll call you if anything changes."

Later, Sy alone in his office, contemplated what to do as he swirled the ice around in his highball glass. He couldn't let go of the idea that Hope was still in pain. That she could hear Sammy's thoughts. That in the afterlife, one was still aware of what was happening here. That the soul never dies. What the psychic had said left him with a grim feeling. His body tensed with a wave of uncertainty about the crossroad between life and death. He tried to concentrate on the file he'd been working on but couldn't. He took off his glasses and rubbed his eyes. He slowly opened his left-hand desk drawer and pulled out Darlene Evans's business card. Pondering for a moment, he lay down the card and looked up a number in his Rolodex and dialed.

"Rabbi, this is your favorite heretic, Syrus Marcus, calling to ask a favor."

Chortling, the rabbi said, "I love a good heretic, Sy; makes my job more interesting. What can I do for you?"

"I'd like to make an appointment to see you about something that's really bothering me—something I can't talk about over the phone."

"I have tomorrow afternoon available at five o'clock if that works for you."

"Thanks, that's great; I'll call if I can't be there by five. Court, you know, I never know when I will get out."

Syrus was glad the next day when the court hearing for his case was moved to a later date; that meant he could get out of the office early. He was anxious about his meeting with the rabbi and wanted to prepare himself, writing down questions and thinking through how much to tell him.

The rabbi smiling, welcomed Sy into his office. They sat down and began to talk. Sy started with the problems in his marriage while the rabbi listened with interest.

When Sy mentioned that he loved his wife but she was driving him crazy with her constant badgering, the rabbi smiled and said, "Tell me what you do love about your wife."

"To me she has always been gorgeous and sexy. The first thing I noticed about her was her smile and her laughter. She has the most melodic laugh. She is courageous, honest, and always there for the family—hers and mine. She's very intelligent and down to earth. She's a wonderful mother; the kids always come first, after me." He chuckled as he continued. "She doesn't have a selfish bone in her body, and she's always been composed. By that I mean she was never quick to react and would listen to reason—until lately. But now she's accusing me of infidelity, and I've never cheated on her. When I'm not working, I'm home unless I'm playing golf."

The rabbi rolled his chair forward as he leaned in, his eyes serious, and in a contemplative voice, he asked, "When you are home, do you spend time with her, or are you bringing your work home with you?"

Sy felt a stab of guilt that surprised him. "I have to work at home or stay at the office. I've taken cases I didn't want to just to provide for my family. My dad worked day and night, and Mom never complained."

"Yes, but times have changed," the rabbi said. "For women, marriage used to be a necessity, but it's not anymore. Now they don't just need a provider; now they want a companion: someone they can have fun with—someone they can talk to."

"We've always had fun together. I think her real problem has to do with Hope's death."

The rabbi, sounding concerned, said, "Yes, Rachel and Hope were so very close. I'm sure it left a huge void in her life. Maybe I could talk to her ... help her to accept Hope's passing ... that her death was only a transition and her soul does live on."

"Rabbi, what does Judaism believe happens to our soul when we die?"

"It's returned to Hashem (God) and, for one year, is judged by him. For that year, the mourners can help to elevate the soul of the deceased by their good deeds, daily prayers, and acts of charity."

"You say our soul is returned to Hashem. What does that mean?"

The rabbi sat back in his chair, folding his arms and looking at the ceiling studiously. Then, gesturing broadly, he reflected. "Let me explain that with my ballpark analogy. You see, everyone gets to go to the game; however, those who have lived a good and moral life get the best seats, closest to Hashem ... for the best insight, the greatest understanding."

"You mean child molesters and mass murderers are in the stadium?"

"Yes, but I like to think of them as being in the back row of the nosebleed section ... where the beer vendors never go." Both men chuckled.

Syrus was intrigued. "So if we all go to heaven, what are we doing with our time that supposedly lasts forever?"

"I believe heaven is the place where our questions are answered—things we're not privy to here because of our limited understanding on earth. I believe we are there to learn more about who we are and our relationship with Hashem."

"Rabbi, do you think the dead can communicate with us through mediums?"

"In the Jewish faith, we are forbidden to consult with a medium. There are many reasons for that. We are not supposed to put our trust in anyone but Hashem, and trust that he will guide us in our lives. We can develop an intuitive understanding of what Hashem wants for each of us through the study of the Torah."

Sy smiled. "I'm going to have to think about that. In the meantime, I'm going to try to get Rachel to meet with you. She really needs your wise counsel. Thanks again for meeting with me on such short notice, Rabbi." He rose and reached his hand out in gratitude.

24

RACHEL TRIED TO EAT SOME OATMEAL, BUT AFTER A FEW BITES, SHE lost her appetite. Her cup of coffee was her only solace. She wanted to be anyone but herself today. Why couldn't she stop being angry? It was ruining her marriage, and now she had no one to talk with. She longed for the days when she and Sy could share their thoughts—any thought. Just when she had begun to believe they were making progress, they'd had the hideous confrontation, and instead of talking about it, he'd cut her off again. She couldn't talk to her mother; just the mention of Hope made her cry. Her friends certainly did not understand, and she wouldn't dare tell them about the psychic; they would for sure think she had lost her mind.

The only person she could talk to was Hope, which meant going back to the psychic. Rachel looked at the clock and realized she had to hurry and shower and get to her shop, as too many women were counting on her. She thought, *Well, the good news is everyone will be happy; they always are when they are being fitted for a beautiful gown for a momentous occasion.* Rachel was grateful. She needed to be around happy people; their euphoric moods always lifted her spirits. She rushed through the morning ritual and dressed in one of her latest creations.

Then she remembered she had actually designed it for Hope, and she plummeted into that dark hole of agony. Suddenly she felt a knowing that Hope was with her, trying to bring her out of the darkness. She looked in the mirror again and could have sworn she saw the shadow of Hope smiling at her as if to say, "It looks good on you too." She picked up the phone and called Darlene.

Rachel preferred not to dwell upon her psychic experiences while at work for fear she would blurt something out insane enough to be noticed. She focused on her work and counted the hours until she could talk to Darlene, who felt as much like a therapist as a psychic. She hoped Darlene might be able to give her insight into what was happening. Was she depressed and escaping from reality, or was it really Hope trying to communicate with her from beyond the grave? She thought about calling a psychiatrist but then thought, *Holy shit, they will give me some drug and lock me up; then I will never get this sorted out.* Even though she was intuitive, that did not make her psychic.

Rachel did remember one time when she was in her early twenties and in college. It was a beautiful spring day, and she was singing along with the radio while driving way too fast as she was coming up to a familiar stop sign at a T intersection—one that she often rolled through. Suddenly it felt as though someone jerked her by the shoulder. It scared her so badly, mainly because no one was in the car with her, that she slammed on her brakes. As she slid into the intersection, a car was coming, travelling at least fifty miles an hour, and they had the right of way. Rachel quickly pulled her car as far out of the other car's path as possible, and they missed each other by only a quarter of an inch. Afterward she pulled over to the side of the road because she shaking and her heart was pounding so hard, she could feel it in her ears.

She knew it sounded absurd, but something had caused her to slam on her brakes; otherwise she would have been in a terrible accident that day and it would have been her fault. That was in the days before seatbelts were in use, so it was likely she would have been killed. That was when she began to believe in guardian angels, as there was no other explanation.

When Rachel arrived at Darlene's, she started telling her about the

114

recurring dreams she was having about Hope. Darlene helped Rachel to understand the dreams. Rachel then told her what had happened that morning.

"When I looked in the mirror, I remembered I had designed this dress for Hope. I started to cry and relapsed into despair. Then the room took on a strange glow, and a feeling of love and joy embraced me. When I looked back at the mirror, I could have sworn, for a brief moment, I saw Hope smiling at me."

Darlene moved forward and leaned in. "Yes, I believe Hope was visiting you, and since you have connected with her here, in this strong vortex of energy, it would not be unusual for her to be able to connect with you anywhere."

Rachel asked, "Would you channel Hope for me again?"

Darlene explained, "I cannot demand a spirit come to me, but I did meditate earlier this morning after you called and asked Hope to be with us. There's no guarantee that she will come through, but I'll try."

They settled into their meditative states, and as soon as Rachel started to meditate, she could feel Hope's essence, a vibration. But it was different from what she had felt before. Hope was coming through in a very emotional state, crying out, "Why did he do this to me! I thought he loved me! I thought I was his best friend!" Rachel watched Darlene in shock as she took on Hope's mannerisms, her way of expressing herself, and even the way she cried out. "I miss you all so much! It was not my time to go; it was not my time to go."

Rachel felt that she needed to be as strong for Hope in the afterlife as she had been in life. Rachel cried out to her, "I'm here, Hope! I'm here for you! I'll help you!"

The psychic collapsed quietly and came out of the trance. She shuddered, opened her eyes, and shook her head. "I couldn't stand the pain she was going through; I had to come out of it. It's not good for me or her when she's like that. I will meditate again later and ask her angels to work to comfort her and tell her we're here to help her find peace."

"Is there anything I can do?"

"Yes, you can meditate and send her love, but you can't cry or be

Sy stepped inside but kept his distance. "I'd like to request the honor of your company next Wednesday night to attend my nephew's wedding. I assume you still plan to go."

"No, I'm not sure I want to go. I'd feel uncomfortable under the circumstances."

"Let's not go public with our problems. I have to go, and I'd really appreciate it if you'd go with me."

"All right, I'll go, but I'm not staying any later than necessary."

"Fine. I'll pick you up at seven."

"No, I'll meet you there, because I'll probably need to pick up Mom."

"Fine. I'll meet you there." Sy smiled half-heartedly as he turned to leave. As soon as he was gone, Rachel dropped into a chair as tears started to roll down her cheeks. She wanted so much to tell him about what had happened today, but she knew it was pointless, given his attitude. She remembered a time when there were no secrets in their marriage, and now it seemed as if everything was a secret.

25

BEFORE SY LEFT HIS OFFICE FOR COURT, HE PICKED UP A MESSAGE LEFT by his law clerk, Marty. Sy was anxious to hear what he had found on the jurisdiction issue. As soon as he was finished with the court hearing, he returned to his office and buzzed Marty's extension.

Soon after, Marty entered Sy's office and handed him a file with a big smile.

"The federal statute says when the death of an American citizen occurs on the high seas on an American vessel and is a suspected murder, jurisdiction can then become the port of entry where the body first enters the United States."

"Yes, so what port did the body come through?"

"That's the great news; Fed Ex flew the body directly from the Bahamas to Memphis. Doesn't that mean we can do an investigation to find out how she died?"

Sy pushed forward so quickly he nearly came out of the chair as he started drumming the desk with glee. "Yes, and that makes it so much easier to get an exhumation order. Thanks, Marty; that'll be all." He picked up the phone and dialed the DA's office and asked for Bryan Ramsey. They worked out a time to meet on Wednesday afternoon.

Sy arrived at Ramsey's office before six and found him on the phone. He waited impatiently, walking back and forth in front of the big glass windows.

Finally, Ramsey waved him in.

"Okay, so fill me in."

Sy started building his case. "Remember what I told you about my sister-in-law's death and the million-dollar life insurance payoff?" Ramsey nodded. "Well, her husband and his business partner, Alfred, are now openly living together as lovers. And Alfred was the only one with her when she died ... and his story doesn't add up."

"Why didn't you mention this on the golf course?"

"Because I wanted to research the jurisdiction issue and be sure it could be tried in Memphis before I pursued it with you."

"You told me, while we were playing golf, Sam Grossman was a respected businessman with no prior record. So what do you want me to do?"

"Order an autopsy; see if it shows foul play. If she was murdered, we'll prosecute."

"You realize if you dig her up and find out she did choke to death, you're opening yourself up for a major lawsuit."

"That's a risk I'll have to take. My wife is obsessed with this; I have to find out how her sister died so she can have closure."

"Even if I agree, I'll need to find a judge who will sign the order."

"Davis might. She knows I don't ask for anything frivolous."

"Yes, but is an autopsy still possible?"

"Yes, I checked with the coroner. He said the sooner the better."

"You know how the statute reads concerning next of kin."

"Her mother and sister will sign."

"What if someone calls the husband?"

"I called his office today, and he's in Europe with Alfie for a month. We need to do it now!"

"But what if the judge—"

Syrus was getting angrier by the minute and finally stood, flushed and fuming. "Come on; you've done more for murderers you knew were guilty ... Bryan, this is really important to me!"

"All right, all right. Calm down; I will see what I can do. I'll try to get a meeting with Judge Davis in the morning. I'll ask her if she'll sign."

Syrus wanted to give him a big hug but instead just shook his hand vigorously. "Thanks, Bryan. I owe you one."

Sy rushed to get home to change clothes and get to the wedding, but it was past 7:00 p.m. when he arrived at the synagogue, and the wedding was already in progress. He spotted Rachel sitting with her mother; the empty seat was next to his mother-in-law. Luckily, they were on the edge of the aisle, so he only had to crawl over Rachel and Sara. Rachel gave him an icy glare as he got to his seat. The wedding party stood under the chuppah, and Rabbi Levy held up the glass wrapped in a white cloth as he spoke.

"As blissfully happy as you are today, understand that marriage, like this glass, is fragile. It reminds us that we do have to work at marriage and that insensitivity, indifference, and selfishness can shatter this sacred union."

Rachel could hardly hold back the tears. Sy moved forward to look at her and smiled knowingly. She turned her head away and tried to disguise her sadness with a pathetic smile, dabbing her teary eyes as if in joy for the couple.

The rabbi put the glass on the floor, and the groom stomped on it.

Everyone joyously pronounced, "Mazel tov!" As the bride and groom made their way up the aisle, the guests all sang and clapped. "Khossen, Kalleh, Mazel tov."

Rachel talked to family and friends during the cocktail party preceding dinner, ignoring Sy. She was surprised she had not seen Sammy, given that the bride's father was his first cousin. Just as dinner was about to be served, Diane and Michael arrived and were seated at their table. Rachel moved over into the empty seat next to Diane and gave her a welcome kiss. "I haven't seen your Dad; is he coming?"

"Oh no, he and Alfie are on a business trip to Europe; they won't be back for another three weeks."

Syrus smiled warmly at Diane and Michael. As the evening wore on, Rachel noticed that he was unusually attentive to both Michael and Diane. He hung on every word Diane said, and as soon as the dinner was finished and the band started playing, he asked Diane to dance with him. As soon as they returned to the table, he asked Rachel to dance. She hesitated, but he was already pulling her from the chair, very insistent. It was a slow dance, and as he tried to pull her in close to him, she rigidly held him at arm's length. He leaned in and whispered, "Don't get too excited, but I did find a life insurance policy on Hope."

"You did?"

"Are you ready for this? Sammy collected over a million dollars."

"Over a million dollars? Mien Gott im Himmel! Now can we do something?"

"Yes, we need to order an autopsy. Your mother can sign the exhumation order, but you're the one who's going to have to explain to her why we're doing this. Are you sure this is what you want to do?"

They continued dancing as Sy filled her in on all the other details of his research. She was flabbergasted to realize he had been doing the research. She pushed back away from him and whispered sharply, "Why didn't you tell me? Was that to get back at me because I made you move out of the house?"

"No, Rachel. I didn't want to get your hopes up. I had to do the legal research to find out if it could even be tried in the state of Tennessee and what it was going to take to do it. I didn't know until yesterday that the body had been flown directly into Memphis. I was trying to make sure I could do something to help; it was not to get even with you for anything."

She hugged him tightly and gave him a grateful smile, though she was still confused. She wished he had talked to her, but the fact that he had gone far enough to request an order to exhume the body was enough for her. At least she would finally have an answer and could get on with her life.

Rachel glanced over at her mother, who was sitting with Diane and Michael. She knew this wasn't going to be easy to explain to anyone, but she had to know the real cause of Hope's death.

The dance ended, and as they walked back toward their table, Syrus stopped her and asked, "Can you talk to your mother tonight?"

"Yes. Mom rode here with me, so I'll talk to her tonight when I take her home. How soon do we need to sign it?"

"I told Ramsey to ask the judge to sign the order based on you and your mother's request. So it could be as soon as tomorrow morning."

As Sy and Rachel reached the table, they smiled at Sara and sat on either side of her. She was always a sharp dresser, and as short as she was, she somehow appeared taller, usually wearing three-inch heels and a hat that gave her extra height. Tonight, was no exception plus she had added her entire collection of diamonds and jewels, including a jeweled hatpin holding her ornate cocktail hat in place. As Sy sat down next to her, she grasped his arm. "Sit, Syrus. Talk to me."

"Sara, you look great. How are you feeling?"

Sara retorted, "Not as good as I look."

Soon after, Sara turned to Rachel to ask when she could take her home.

Rachel replied, "I'm ready when you're ready; just say the word."

Less than five minutes later, Sara said, "I'm ready to go; I've got to get out of these shoes. They're too tight on my feet. I must have bought them when I went on that diet and lost five pounds."

Rachel quickly said her goodbyes to everyone.

While driving her mother home, she tried to prepare her for what she was going to ask her to do. She told her mother that she never felt right about how Hope died—that something always felt strange to her. Sara agreed and said, "I do not trust Sammy. He has changed over the years, and since Hope's death he's even stranger. I have a feeling he had something to do with her death. I just don't know what." Sara remembered when Sammy saw her at the hospital after Hope's cancer surgery. He had fawned over Hope and told Sara how much the family meant to him and how grateful he was for all their help with his beloved wife. Then he left town the next day, not saying anything to anyone but his daughter. He was gone for two weeks, and Hope was depressed and felt neglected. Sara was astonished by the about face of his concern. After a pause, she very matter-of-factly said, "He is the master of duplicity."

Rachel was surprised to hear this from her mother, because she was never one to gossip or to say anything harsh about a family member.

When they arrived at Sara's house, Rachel walked her mother inside, as she had done since her father's passing two years prior. Sara immediately went into the den, took off her shoes, put her feet up on the cocktail table in front of her, and let out a big sigh of relief. Rachel sat in a chair nearby and leaned in. "Mom, I need your help with something that you might think is a little crazy, but I have to do it."

"So tell me what a little crazy is?"

Rachel couldn't think of any nice way to put it, so she just blurted it out. "I want to have Hope's body exhumed so we can have an autopsy done. I have to know how she really died. I don't believe she choked to death."

For a moment, Sara set quietly. Then she said, "So you think he killed her too?"

After the shock of her mother's shared suspicion abated, Rachel realized that she and her mother had not spoken about Sammy since Hope's death. She hesitated to answer as she thought about how much she wanted to divulge to her mother.

"I don't know for sure, but Alfred was there; surely he could have done something. The fact that she died outside the United States is suspicious because that makes it much harder to investigate. Sy has been checking into it, and they didn't do an autopsy, which is very unusual, because Sammy had a million-dollar life insurance policy on her, and insurance companies rarely pay without an autopsy. But the good news is they had to embalm her body before flying her back, so we can still do an autopsy. I just want to know how she really died. I need you to sign the exhumation order with me. Will you do that?"

Sara sat back. Tears filled her eyes as she shrieked, "So that meshugha schmuck got a million dollars?"

"Yes, and he got the inheritance from Dad too, because she had his name as the beneficiary on the account in case of death."

Tears flowed down Sara's face. "What paper do you want me to sign?"

"Sy said he will call me as soon as he finds out if the judge agrees to sign the order. I hope that it will be tomorrow. If it is, we'll have to drop everything and get down to the DA's office to sign it."

Sara clenched her jaw, pursing her lips. "Good. I'll be ready."

Two days later, Sy called them to come downtown to sign the papers for the exhumation order. Soon after, Sy gave Rachel the day and time to be at the cemetery and asked her to let him know whether everything went as planned.

Rachel winced. "I just hope Diane doesn't go out to the grave and see it has been dug up."

"If she does, you'll have to explain it to her. I'm at a loss for words as to how to explain it.

"I know, I know. I'll handle it if it comes to that."

As soon as Rachel got off the phone, she headed to the master bedroom, where she kept her Valium. When she picked up the empty bottle, it dawned on her she had forgotten to call for a refill. She had to have it; if not for the Valium, she didn't know if she would ever sleep. She called the doctor's office from the phone by the bed. She was tired but didn't want to lie in the bed; she wanted to meditate, hoping it would calm her down. She went to the chaise longue, fluffed up the pillows, and nestled into a cloud of down comfort. She was getting better at meditating, and she hoped it would calm her enough to relax and let go of all the craziness in her life. Her head was pounding. She had been up most of the night worried about her husband, her marriage, and, most of all, the outcome of the autopsy. As she breathed deeply, counting her breaths, she began to feel better, and soon she was asleep.

27

A FEW DAYS LATER, AS SY WAS LEAVING COURT WITH HIS CLIENT, THE DA, Bryan Ramsey, approached him waving a manila envelope. Sy turned to his client. "Excuse me a minute; I need to see what the DA wants. Just take a seat." He pointed to the benches farther down the hall.

Ramsey motioned Sy into a nearby office. Sy grabbed the envelope and ripped it open.

As Sy scanned the report, his jaw clenched and his whole body grew rigid. For a moment he felt he was going to collapse. In a stupor he took hold of a chair, his mind reeling. "Cyanide? My God, I can't believe this. She went through so much with the cancer … fought so hard to live. How could they have done this to her?"

"Apparently the million dollars meant more to them. And you said the husband inherited everything else as well, right?"

Sy's breathing was shallow, and his hands shook. "Yes, he did. There were three life insurance policies plus Hope's inheritance, which was over three hundred thousand dollars in an account with him as the beneficiary. On top of that, the million-dollar policy had a double indemnity clause, so it's possible he got two million dollars. Greed is such a cruel master." Sy wiped away tears and tried to compose himself. "You have no idea what a sweetheart she was; everybody loved her."

"Yeah, well, there's a giant line between love and psycho killers."

"Yes, how soon can we get these two charged with murder?"

"Hold on, Sy; this is a real long shot. It's all circumstantial. You're going to have to get me some hard evidence before I can pursue this. My office doesn't have the time or staff this case will require."

"Can't you appoint a special prosecutor?"

"Yeah, you. You're one of the best prosecutors to come out of this office."

Sy shook his head. "It's been a long time since I sat on that side of the courtroom."

"It'd be a pleasure having you on my side of the courtroom for a change."

Sy paced the room, looking at the report. "I don't know if I could be objective. This is my family. My wife may have to testify."

"No problem; I'll try it with you myself. But I don't have time to prepare the case; you'll have to do it."

The two men stared at each other. Sy slapped the report on the table and shook his head. "I can't believe they thought they could murder Hope right under *my* nose and get away with it."

"A hum, justice takes on a whole new meaning when it hits close to home, doesn't it, Sy?"

His face was red with rage. Holding the documents, he raised his hand, as if swearing to God, "Yes, and those two are going to learn a whole new meaning to the word 'justice.' Crazed he slammed the file on the desk as he said, "I'll see to it. That soulless bastard Sammy is going to answer to me for what he did!"

Bryan clapped a hand on Sy's shoulder. "Now that's the Sy I like to see. I'll back you all the way. Let's nail the bastards!"

"Yes, let's do it. It's unbelievable." Sy shook his head, remembering how Rachel had pleaded for his help, and he knew he owed her more than an apology. She deserved the very best defense for her sister. Sy lamented, "We're going to teach him and his lackey a lesson they'll never forget!" He walked out, slamming the door behind him. Everyone in the hallway moved out of his way, his fury obvious, as he stalked toward his client.

28

Sy called Rachel after he returned to his office. "Rachel, we need to meet for dinner tonight. How about the Half Shell?"

Rachel said, "Sure, what's up? Did you get the results from the autopsy?"

"Not yet, but we need to discuss the possibilities if they do show that Hope was poisoned."

"Honey, I appreciate what you have done. It doesn't matter anymore what the outcome is, just that there is one. I promise that if the autopsy shows she died from choking, I will never go to a psychic again and I will get into grief counseling for as long as it takes for me to heal."

Sy muttered, "Honey, I know how difficult this has been for you, and I'm sorry I was not more supportive. It was all a shock to me too. I know I didn't handle it well. Do me a favor; try to get to the restaurant early and get a corner table away from other people. I don't want people listening in. Okay?"

"Sure. I'll see you there."

Sy ran through all the possible scenarios of the murder trial as he drove to the restaurant to meet Rachel. He had lied to her because he wanted time to think it through before saying anything. He was still struggling with the idea that Sammy could actually have planned to murder Hope. He had always talked out of both sides of his mouth and was probably a sex addict—but a murderer? That was quite a stretch. Alfie must have done it, but Alfie was such a wimp Sy couldn't fathom that he was capable of doing such a horrific thing. Sammy had to be the mastermind. Still, Sy felt there was something missing; there had to be more to it than just the money. There was plenty of money in the family to help Sammy.

He was heartsick knowing the hardest thing he could imagine was yet to come; he had to tell Rachel that her sister had been murdered. Sy's apprehension was making him question his own ability to deal with the situation. His heart was pounding; he was shaky, and his stomach was tied in knots. For one of the few times in his life, he felt emotionally off balance. But he had to remain stoic, because it was going to take every ounce of strength he could summon, to not break down, when he tells Rachel the truth.

When he entered the restaurant, he spotted her in a far corner booth, close to the window. She saw him coming. He knew her joyous smile and enthusiastic waving would not last for long. He was glad there was a drink waiting for him.

As he slid into the booth across from her, Rachel pounced. "So what's going on? What? What?"

He took a drink before saying, "I got the autopsy report back today." He hesitated and took a deep breath. He took both her hands in his as he said softly, "Hope had enough cyanide in her to kill two people."

Time stopped. Rachel couldn't breathe, and for a moment she thought she was going to collapse, but she could hear herself stammer, "Oh my God. How could he? What kind of monster is he?"

"I'm sure he and Alfie were in on it together, because Alfie was the one who had to give her the poison, somehow. You know they think they've gotten away with it ... the perfect murder."

Still in a stupor and fighting back tears, she whispered, "You're not going to let them get away with this, are you?"

"Hell no! They're not getting away with anything. Ramsey is going to appoint me special prosecutor."

Rachel was so grateful she jumped from her seat and hugged him, whispering, "Oh Sy, you're so amazing, so brilliant; no one could do this but you." Relieved, he patted her back.

Rachel sat back down and took a sip of her martini. She sat quietly, grief-stricken and shaking, wiping away tears as quickly as they appeared. Sy waved the waiter over and ordered both another drink. After the waiter left, she took his hand, "Oh God, Sy, what am I going to say to Diane? How do I tell her?"

"You can't tell her anything—not yet. We have to get Sammy and Alfred back to Memphis; no one can know who might warn them. You cannot say anything to anyone—especially the psychic; I don't trust her."

"Really, Sy, you don't want to go there with me. If it were not for her, we'd never have known Hope was murdered."

"Keep your voice down. If you tell anyone about that psychic, it will ruin my credibility. As far as anyone knows, you remembered Hope told you about the insurance policy; you just didn't remember when or how much—which is what I told Ramsey. Let's keep it that way, okay?"

"Yes, but I have to see the psychic again. I want to talk to Hope. Maybe there's information she can give us that will help with the case."

Sy's jaw tightened, and with an intense growl he replied, "No. You *cannot* do that. If you do, I will drop the case and not pursue it at all. Do not contact her under any circumstances; do you understand me?"

Rachel leaned in, frowning. "But what if there's more information she can give us to help out with the trial?"

"No. For the last time, I'm telling you … stay away from her. I have detectives that can find evidence we can actually use in court. Besides, once this is announced to the media, they will be watching every move we make. At that point it would only make matters worse if you involve that psychic."

"Okay, I understand. I just wanted to help. But I'll do whatever you say."

29

Syrus followed the patrol car to Memphis International Airport to apprehend Sammy and Alfred. He had given them a thorough description of both men and filled them in about the men who had allegedly murdered his sister-in-law. When they arrived at the airport, he and the two officers entered the terminal together. They checked for the arrival gate on a monitor and proceeded to the gate. Sy stood near the Jetway where the arriving passengers were deplaning. Sammy and Alfie were among the first to get off the plane. When Sy spotted them, he signaled the officers, who moved in for the arrest as he stepped into the background to observe.

Officer Morrow stopped the two men. "Samuel Grossman? Alfred Birmingham?"

Both men looked back with blank stares and stood rigid as they nodded.

The second officer stepped forward with handcuffs ready. Officer Morrow pronounced loudly enough for everyone nearby to hear, "You're under arrest for the murder of Hope Grossman."

As the second officer put handcuffs on each one, he read them their Miranda rights. "You have the right to remain silent ..."

Only Sammy spoke as he turned to face Alfred. "Don't say one word; I will call my lawyer as soon as we get to the police station. Say absolutely nothing; my lawyer will have us out in no time."

As they were being led down the corridor, Syrus stepped out of the crowd to join them. At first Sammy thought he saw a friendly face and smiled. "Sy, what's going on here?"

Sy stepped directly in front of Sammy. "Did you really think you'd get away with killing Hope? You greedy, rotten son of a bitch. Have you gone completely mad? You couldn't just divorce her?"

Sammy, equally incensed, cried out, "What are you talking about? Have you lost your mind? And what the hell do you have to do with this?"

"We know you poisoned her, and I'm going to prove it!"

The officers jerked Sammy away and continued down the corridor. Sammy was livid as he turned to Alfred and spewed, "Don't worry; I'll teach that pompous ass a thing or two about the law."

The clamor of the police headquarters was the last thing Sammy had imagined he would have to deal with upon their return. He was still in shock when they arrived at the booking area. As he answered the officers' questions and emptied his pockets, all he could think was that he had to call his lawyer. He kept asking repeatedly for permission to call his lawyer until finally they directed him to the phone. As he dialed the number, he realized for the first time that he was shaking uncontrollably. Alfred was waiting nervously nearby as Sammy made the call. The booking area was noisy, dirty, and filled with unsavory criminals and homeless drunks. Alfred, who had never been in a police station in his entire life, looked around in disbelief that this could be happening to him. He moved closer to Sammy, listening in on the phone conversation. Sammy had apparently reached a stubborn secretary, and he was practically screaming, "Let me speak to Wayne Emmons now. It's urgent! *No!* I cannot call him back … I'm at the police station. Tell him it's Samuel Grossman and it's an emergency. I've been arrested!"

Emmons came on the line. "Sammy, what's the big emergency?"

"You have to get down here right now and get us out of jail!"

"What are *you* doing in jail?"

"They've charged Alfred and me with first-degree murder!"

"Murder? Who're they accusing you of murdering?"

"My wife, Hope." Sammy looked over at Alfred to see him looking pale and shaky. "I don't care what it costs; just get us out of here."

"Sammy, I would if I could, but it's too late today. No judge'll set a bond by phone for murder one."

"There must be something you can do?"

"I'll call a judge right away and get something set for first thing in the morning. Just calm down; as soon as I finish here, I'll get down there to see you. Do not talk to the detectives until I get there; refuse to say anything—got it?"

Sammy was still shaking as he hung up the phone. He turned to Alfred. Two white skinheads in dirty fatigues and handcuffs looked Alfred up and down. One moved closer to him and, with a sly smile, asked, "Is those I-talian shoes?"

Alfie looked down at his shoes and, in a huff, turned his back on the man. The officer came to take them to their cell for their overnight stay in jail. Sammy was incensed as he complained to the officer, "We are not common criminals; this has all been a misunderstanding. We did not kill anyone. Do not put us in one of those filthy cells. We want a clean one for just the two of us. We have to stay together." The officer smirked. "Sure, don't worry; we'll get you a cell as fine as the Ritz."

Alfred chimed in. "Officer, sir, we'll cooperate, and I don't care about a clean cell, but please, we have to stay together." The officer just looked at them in amusement.

The next morning, Syrus Marcus and District Attorney Bryan Ramsey entered the courtroom where the bond hearing was being held. Sammy and Alfred looked as though they had slept in their clothes as they talked quietly with their attorney, Wayne Emmons. Emmons had already arranged for the bail bondsman to meet with him before the hearing to get the paperwork done, so they would be able to post bond immediately after the hearing.

As soon as the court was called to order, the judge listened politely as each side argued its opinion. It took only a few minutes for the judge to decide.

"Bond is set at two hundred fifty thousand dollars each. They're not to leave Shelby County for any reason before the trial—understood?"

Emmons said, "Yes, Your Honor."

A brigade of press and TV cameras waited to ambush Sammy, Alfred, and Emmons as they tried to leave the courtroom. Emmons said, "No comment," as he and another attorney pushed his clients through the crowd into the office to post their bond.

DA Bryan Ramsey and Sy Marcus tried to escape in the confusion but were spotted by the Nose for News, reporter Don Heller. He directed everyone to follow him as he ran over to confront Syrus.

"Mr. Marcus, you're a highly paid defense attorney. Why were you appointed special prosecutor?"

Sy stepped forward, stood taller, and took a deep breath before answering. "The prosecutor's office is overworked and backlogged. In the fine state of Tennessee, a victim's family has the right to hire an attorney as a special prosecutor if the DA approves."

"Yes, but isn't the murder victim your sister-in-law? Wouldn't that be a conflict of interest for you to prosecute your own brother-in-law?"

"No, I have a right to see justice is done, just as any other citizen does."

All the reporters started shouting questions at once as Sy and Bryan turned and walked away yelling, "No comment!" They quickly moved to an elevator around the corner. As they stood alone waiting, they discussed the case. Bryan asked, "Syrus, where did you get the information on the insurance policy?"

"Remember I told you that Hope told Rachel about getting a big life insurance policy, but she didn't remember what company or how much. At first when she asked me to look into it, I thought, 'What does it matter?' I decided I wouldn't do it. But then she ran into a psychic and asked her about the insurance. And of course, the psychic said a big policy had been taken out on her life. After that, Rachel was driving me crazy, saying the psychic told her she had to look into it. So I had my detective research it, and he found the million-dollar policy as well as two other policies."

"Your wife got the info from a psychic?"

"Yes, it was Darlene Evans, the one who worked on the Turner case with the police. So at least she is reputable."

"Yes, I know who she is, but let's not tell anyone about that; it won't help our case any."

"No, of course not, and I've already instructed my wife not to talk about it to anyone. She promised me she wouldn't."

The elevator doors opened, and they stepped inside. As the elevator doors closed, the reporter Don Heller stepped out of the shadows, writing on his pad while smiling to himself.

30

SAMMY AND ALFRED MADE THEIR WAY TO THEIR ATTORNEY'S OFFICE on the tenth floor of the Bank of the South building in downtown Memphis. "Let me do all the talking, Alfie. You can't let anything he says upset you. If he asks you anything, just keep saying, 'I didn't do anything! I tried to save her!' Don't get into any long explanation. Our side of the story needs to be honest and straightforward. Can you handle that without getting upset?"

Alfred stood straight, held his head erect, and stared down at his manicured fingernails as he nodded. "I'm fine; your worrying that I don't know how to act is bothering me more than anything else. I had years of practice when I was in the closet. So just stop it, darling, or I'll have a little hissy fit right in front of him."

"Okay, okay, I get it."

They entered the door into a lobby that looked like something out of *Architectural Digest*, very sleek and modern with rich colors. A stainless steel cantilevered desk centered the room. Prominently located above the desk was the name of the law firm in bold stainless steel letters. The lighting was unusual, from the spotlights in the ceiling to the ambient lighting emanating from the floor, casting shadows of the plants on the wall in artistic display, with pictures positioned perfectly between the shadows. Alfred was impressed as he looked around. "Well, he certainly has good taste."

Sammy nodded as he talked to the receptionist. "We have an appointment with Wayne Emmons. I'm Samuel Grossman."

"Yes, Mr. Grossman, I'll call his secretary; she'll take you back to his office."

Within minutes, an older heavyset woman with huge earrings and huge hair to match introduced herself as Sue Ellen, Mr. Emmons's secretary. They followed her down a long hallway to a set of double doors. As they entered, Emmons rose to greet them. He shook Sammy's hand first and then extended his hand to Alfred. As Emmons quickly withdrew his hand, he motioned his clients toward the chairs. Sammy sat down and blurted, "What's this all about, Wayne?"

Emmons settled into his cushy leather chair and took a deep breath. He pushed himself backward in his chair, first glancing out the window and then moving forward to focus on the open file on his desk.

Wayne sternly stated, "This is not a frivolous lawsuit. The DA has some strong circumstantial evidence. They've exhumed Hope's body and performed an autopsy."

Furious, Sammy exclaimed, "How could they exhume Hope's body without my permission?"

Emmons picked up the file on his desk and read. "They could and they did, with a judge's order, based on the first next of kin being the possible suspect in the victim's death. Then it says here they found a large quantity of cyanide in her body and that *you* collected two million dollars from a life insurance policy. They also allege that you and your … partner here are living together as lovers, and that Alfred was the only one with Hope when she died." Emmons leaned forward, forcefully tapping on the desk in front of Sammy as he demanded, "Now how much of this is true?"

Sammy shook his head in disbelief. He looked at Alfie, who had lost all color while gripping the chair arms and leaning forward as if he were about to vomit. Sammy reached over, gripped his arm, and gave him a reassuring look.

As Sam turned back to Emmons, he said, "Only the part about the life insurance is true."

"Uh huh. So Sam, I understand you were in Memphis at the time of your wife's death."

"Yes. Yes, I was."

Emmons charged ahead. "All right then, first we have to deal with a potential conflict of interest. I can't represent both of you. I recommend we get another attorney for Mr. Birmingham."

Alfred leaned forward and grabbed Sammy's arm. "You said we'd have the same attorney."

Sammy pulled his arm away from Alfie. "Wayne is the expert here. We have to listen to what he advises us to do."

"I can recommend several good attorneys."

"We'll trust your judgment. After all, neither one of us has broken a law—not even the speed limit—in years."

Alfred, shaking his head vigorously, agreed.

"Okay, Sam, I need to speak with you alone."

"No, it's okay; I want Alfred here. There's nothing to hide, I assure you."

"All right, it's your decision. But Sam, I've got to know the truth. Are you guilty or not?"

"I told you *I'm* not guilty, and neither is Alfred."

"You know I'm still gonna conduct my own investigation. If I find your story doesn't jibe with the facts and you start changing it midstream, it's gonna affect your defense."

Sammy blustered. "Don't worry; the story will match the facts."

"Yeah ... if you were guilty, we'd have a different game plan. You'd still have a trial, but I would not put you on the witness stand to lie."

"Wayne, I had nothing to do with her death! We were married over twenty-eight years ... Honest to God, I could never hurt her. I loved her."

"Then give me something I can use to help you prove it."

"I was hoping this would never have to come out. It'll hurt a lot of people ... especially our daughter. But here goes."

Sammy began relating the story to Emmons. As Sammy finished his story, Emmons looked relieved, although not entirely convinced.

"This has all been a huge misunderstanding, but I want you to put Syrus Marcus in his place," Sammy said. "I can't believe he didn't just talk to me instead of filing murder charges against me. It's *outrageous!*"

"Well, if what you told me is true, we may beat this."

Sammy glared at Alfred as he sternly commanded, "Alfred, sit still and listen, would you? You're making me nervous with your fidgeting. Did you hear him? He just said we'd beat this."

Alfred quickly sat up straight in his chair, smiling unwillingly.

"Hold on, Sammy; let me make this clear. You and Alfred are charged with *both* first-degree murder *and* conspiracy to commit first-degree murder. The maximum penalty is death by electrocution or life in prison. This is as serious as it gets!"

"You don't really think we could be convicted, do you?"

"I damn sure do! If you don't listen to me and do exactly as I say … you're *damn right* you could be convicted!"

Sammy got quiet, and Alfred wilted in his chair.

"What do you want us to do?" Sammy asked.

"First, get the hell out of Alfred's house. Get your own place. Second, don't discuss this case with anyone, anytime, for any reason. Third, quit looking like a couple. Do you understand? Sam, get a date with a woman, and if possible, screw her publicly, like in the lobby bar at the Peabody Hotel. You get the drift?"

"Yeah, I got it."

"Do you really think that's necessary?" Alfred asked in a strained voice.

Wayne looked at him as he shook his head. "Look, I don't care about a person's sexual preference … but we have to be realistic. We're in the Bible Belt … Hell, Memphis is the *buckle* of the Bible Belt, and you're not gonna get much sympathy from a jury if they think you're a couple."

"Wayne, we're business partners, nothing more. I'm as straight as you are."

Emmons got up and escorted them to the door as he blatantly replied, "Yeah, well, it's everyone else you need to convince, not me."

31

Soon after Sammy and Alfred left, Emmons pressed the intercom button, putting on his suit coat as he spoke. "Sue Ellen, call Jim Lockard. See if he can meet me tonight at six at the Rum Boogie Bar on Beale Street. Tell him I have a client for him on a real important case. I've got to get to court. If Jim can't meet tonight, send a law clerk over to let me know. Thanks."

Later Emmons got word that Jim could meet with him. As he walked down the street toward the Rum Boogie Bar, he spotted Jim Lockard crossing the street. Lockard waved as he waited by the door. They shook hands and entered the bar together. They stood for a moment to let their eyes adjust to the darkness before choosing a table in a far corner away from the patrons, most of whom were sitting at the bar. Lockard was a few years younger than Emmons, but his beard made him appear older and wiser. The waiter took their drink orders, and as soon as he walked away, Emmons started giving Lockard details of the case.

Perplexed Lockard said, "You've known Sammy fifteen years, and you didn't know he was possibly gay?"

"Jesus, how would I know? The only time I saw him was at social events with his wife. Besides, he insists he's straight."

"So what's your defense strategy?"

"I think the worst thing we could do is to put Alfred Birmingham on the stand."

"Right. From your description, he could hurt us just walking to the stand."

"Yeah, even if he's innocent, they'd hang him by his little twinkle toes. So now Jim, you sure you won't have any problem defending a homo?"

"No. Just because he's a little light in the loafers doesn't make him a criminal. I'll never understand homos, but it is what it is. So where do we start?"

"There's an investigative reporter meeting us here, supposedly has some information we could use; I don't know what it's about."

"Who is it?"

"Don Heller from the *Daily News*. Jim, the first thing I'm going to check out is the investigation done in the Bahamas—see if it jibes with Sammy's story."

"She died in the Bahamas? How can they even try it in Memphis?

"Good point, Lockard, my man. I'm getting the research done on that as soon as possible."

Don Heller entered the bar and spotted Emmons and Lockard across the room. He headed to their table in the corner and dropped a manila envelope in front of Emmons.

"I'll be covering the case. If I run across anything else, I'll call you."

Emmons nodded. "Okay. Thanks, buddy."

As quickly as he had come, he was gone. Emmons opened the envelope and pulled out several sheets with newspaper clippings attached. After reading for a minute, he looked up at Lockard and shook his head. "He says they got info on the murder from a psychic and he has some articles on her. I don't know what this has to do with anything. I was hoping he had something on the rumored homosexual angle. This brings me to a very important point. When you meet with Mr. Birmingham—and try to meet with him alone if there is any way possible—see if you can get any insight into his relationship with Sam. Alfred acted like a jealous girlfriend. We need to make sure there are no pictures or love letters out there that prove he is."

"Okay, I'll see what I can ferret out of him." They finished their drinks and their conversation and left the now noisy and crowded bar.

32

Syrus sat at his desk, tapping his pen while reading and rereading the report from the Bahamian police chief. The report said very little except that there had been a thorough investigation, whatever that meant. Syrus had tried for weeks to get information on the coroner who had examined Hope's body. No one seemed to know anything except that he had left and had taken a job back in India. He had left no forwarding address or phone number, which was strange.

It looked more and more like a premeditated murder. If only they could find the coroner in India, but it was near impossible because his last name was Singh, which was the last name for half the country. They could offer him immunity if he would testify and tell the truth. That alone could give them the winning hand.

Sam and Alfred must have gone to Nassau before the murder and made arrangements to pay the coroner when the time came. But how did Alfred get Hope to take the poison? Did he put it in her coffee or in the cream cheese on her bagel? Sy doubted he put it in her coffee, because it would have tasted bitter, so maybe orange juice; that would be a better choice for cyanide. This murder was meticulously planned, and he was going to have to send a detective to the Bahamas to do some digging. There had to be a file on Hope's death and on the embalming, as well as the paperwork to release the body to US authorities.

When Sy asked for the documents from the Bahamian officials, they claimed they would have to have come from the United States Customs Service. The police report they sent said the body was flown from Bimini to Paradise Island and put in refrigeration until the following Monday because no one worked on the weekend unless it was considered an emergency. Alfred had stayed in Nassau. He had to have met with the coroner early on Monday to prevent him from doing an autopsy. That would have given him the weekend to get with the coroner and buy him off. Sy knew Alfie had flown in on the same morning as Hope's body, because he had signed the customs paperwork. Also, he was the one who had made all the arrangements with the United States Customs Service allowing Fed Ex to ship the body to Memphis.

This case was far more complicated than Sy had anticipated, and he was going to have to pay a lot of money to get a first-rate detective to go to the Bahamas to investigate, but would have to do it if he was going to win this case. The district attorney's office was not going to help with the expense, which was something Ramsey had made quite clear when he agreed to take on the monumental task of trying this case. The partners in Sy's law firm were not happy either. A few of the lawyers in the firm had to cover Sy's other cases and make court appearances to delay important cases. The stress level for Sy had gone through the roof since this started. Everything about this case was maddening, but he couldn't let that get to him; he never had before. In this case, the difference came down to one dramatic fact: Sammy was a relative, and it involved Rachel's entire family—all six aunts and uncles and their families. And they all had opinions about it. None of them could have known how difficult this was for him. Even he questioned his emotions and his ability to stay focused on winning, which was all that mattered at this point.

33

Syrus called Ramsey. "Bryan, I just received the notice from your office that you've set the trial in seven weeks, which is great, but we need to get together soon. Today I received information from my detective that the million-dollar double indemnity policy has paid out two million dollars to Sammy. I've also hired a detective from Nassau to investigate the coroner's office and to track down the coroner who filled out and signed the death certificate, as well as to check into any possible corruption in the coroner's office involving the police department— especially Sgt. Warren, the lead detective."

"When do you expect to get results from him?"

"I called him this morning and told him we needed the info as soon as possible, because we were going to trial in six weeks."

"Good. Let's hope he finds the coroner, but if he's in another country, we're going to have a difficult time getting him to America unless he cooperates with the authorities. I have my doubts he'll cooperate— unless the death certificate has been forged, which is another possibility.

"Right. We also need to set a time to meet with Rachel to work on her testimony. She will be one of our star witnesses, and you'll have to do the questioning. Would you mind coming to our house? I could have Rachel fix dinner. We'd have the privacy to freely discuss the case."

"Fine, that would allow us more time. When did you have in mind?"

They settled on Thursday.

Rachel was ecstatic when Sy told her they would be meeting with Ramsey to discuss her testimony.

On Thursday night, Sy answered the knock at the door and welcomed Bryan Ramsey inside. The smell of barbecue filled the house.

"Smells good."

"Rachel didn't have time to cook, so we picked up some of our favorite barbecue from Corky's. We have a little of everything; hope that's okay."

"Are you kiddin'? Corky's is one of my favorites."

"I'm having a beer; what would you like to drink?"

"A cold beer sounds good."

Sy motioned for him to follow. "Come on into the kitchen; we'll eat in here, and then afterward we'll go into my office to work on the case. Rachel will be down in a minute."

Rachel had heard the doorbell ring and knew the DA arrived. She quickly finished her makeup and rushed downstairs to meet him. She could see within minutes of meeting him what Sy had recognized in him. He was a tall, broad-shouldered, powerful-looking man with a gracious smile that could have won over a fire-eating dragon. Rachel was smiling from ear to ear as she emptied the cartons of barbecue and side dishes into serving bowls and platters. Turning to Bryan, she said, "My husband has good insight into the opposing attorneys; he studies them. He says Wayne Emmons is one of the best lawyers in town. What do you think of Sammy and Alfred's defense team?"

"Both lawyers are great, but they have only a few options for a defense. One would be to blame someone else on the ship; another would be to blame the victim. I'm going with the first option."

Syrus chimed in. "Yeah, Hope's friend Sharon Chamliss is a possibility. What do you know about her, Rachel?"

Rachel said, "Let's eat. I'll tell you what I know when we sit down to go over your strategy and my testimony. I don't want the food to get cold."

Bryan nodded, and Sy pushed the platter of meat toward him. Laughing he said, "You first; I ate some before you got here." Sy and Rachel both catered to Bryan as they passed the food to him, happy they could have the meeting in their home.

After they finished eating, Rachel made coffee and arranged a plate of brownies and cookies for them to nosh on. The guys had gone into the den to check on the Tennessee Vols game against Alabama. Many years before, Rachel had mastered tuning out the TV so she could hear the conversations going on in the den. She could tell more about what they were expressing by the intonation and timbre of their voices, generally, than when she was looking right at them.

Syrus asked, "What do you think of the judge we drew?"

Bryan put his hands together under his chin as he leaned forward. "Gary Maxfield knows his law. Goes by the book … the Good Book."

Syrus nodded. "True, the few times he gets reversed are when he starts thinking more about the Bible than the rules of law. That could work for us or against us, which is why I want to keep the gay issue played down as much as possible. As devious as Sammy is, I wouldn't put it past him to use Alfred as his fall guy."

Rachel joined them, carrying the tray holding coffee and dessert. Sy and Bryan quickly rose to follow her to Sy's home office. Before Rachel could even serve the coffee, Ramsey asked, "What can you tell us about Sharon? Do you know anything about her relationship with Sammy?"

Rachel thought for a moment before responding. "I know she is working with Sammy on the brownstone project as a sales agent, although she said she worked with Alfred on the brownstones most of the time. Sammy and Sharon didn't seem that close until after Hope died. The gossip around town is they are dating, but I've never seen them together. And gossip is not reliable; who knows who's making up what story, and it always gets worse as the story gets passed around. I did go to dinner with her one night and asked her about Sammy, but she claimed she had only met with him to talk about the sale of their house. She seemed annoyed that he spent most of his time with Alfred.

I couldn't tell if she was lying or acting. If she is having an affair with Sammy, she's not going to let anyone know. She was close to Hope. They were roommates in college and stayed in touch through the years. She appeared to be sincerely bereaved at Hope's death. She was on the yacht with her and had spent the morning talking to Hope before going back to her cabin to prepare to leave the yacht. I talked to her at length, and I believe she truly was distraught over Hope's death."

"Okay. Tell me everything you can about Hope and Sammy's relationship: what they fought about, problems they had—anything you think is pertinent in making our case. However, please let us determine what we can and cannot use, okay?"

She nodded. "They appeared to have a perfect marriage, but that was more for show."

"Please explain what you mean by that."

Rachel took a deep breath before starting. "Sammy has a Jekyll and Hyde personality. He could give the impression of being the attentive, caring husband in public, but transformed into a monster the minute they got behind closed doors." Rachel went over the problems she had seen and heard from Hope about her volatile relationship with Sammy over the years.

Ramsey questioned her as if he were the defense attorney. "You claim Hope was planning on divorcing Sammy, then why would she go on the trip to celebrate their anniversary?"

"Sammy pressured her to go, claiming he wanted to do whatever it took to save their marriage."

Both Ramsey and Sy objected. Ramsey said, "That will help the defense. You need to just say Sammy pressured her to go and Hope was afraid that if she refused, he would be furious with her and make her life miserable."

Rachel nodded. "Yes, that's true."

Sy switched to playing the defense attorney. "In your opinion, why did Sammy throw her an expensive and elaborate birthday party weeks before her death?"

Rachel said, "I don't know."

Sy said, "This is where you can make a comment like 'Maybe when you're planning a murder you attempt to mislead everyone, especially the victim.' Of course, the defense will scream objection, but it will be too late. The idea will be heard."

They continued questioning her well past midnight. They did their best to upset her, but she stood her ground, defiantly defending Hope. They were all exhausted by the time the session ended. Before leaving, Ramsey set another time to get together and discuss her testimony further.

After Ramsey left, Sy stopped Rachel before she headed to bed. "I'm doing what you asked me to do, and I want to move back into the house."

Rachel was so tired she did not want to argue. She nodded. "All right, but we still have a lot of other issues to resolve. Go ahead and move into the guest room downstairs. It has a full bath, so it will be convenient for you."

He stopped Rachel and held her by the shoulders as he asked, "Do you want to see a family therapist again, or the rabbi?"

She was emotionally exhausted and simply didn't have the energy to deal with anything else. "I'm so tired; can we please talk about this later? I'll make Shabbat dinner Friday night; if you'll come home, we can talk about it then."

"Fine, but I'm sleeping in the guest room tonight, and I'm moving my stuff back into the house tomorrow, before Jason and Mindy get home this weekend."

"That's fine. Let's keep the kids out of it until we can make a decision about what we're going to do. Good night."

34

SAMMY WAS WITH SHARON HAVING DRINKS IN THE PEABODY HOTEL lobby bar. He waved and got up to talk to anyone and everyone he knew. His picture had made the front page, so he had attained a local celebrity status. Sharon noticed that he was enjoying being the center of attention and felt he was fine being seen with her in public.

Putting his hand on Sharon's, he leaned in to whisper to her, "Darling, because you were on the yacht with Hope and Alfie, I'll need you as a witness. You'll help me, won't you?"

"Now, honey, you just might have to beat me into submission."

Sammy dug his perfectly manicured nails into her thigh as she leaned in closer to him. Sammy said under his breath, "I want you to meet with my lawyers next week. They'll tell you exactly what to say and what not say, okay?"

"Sammy, honey, you know I will. Can we go back to my place and discuss this in more detail? I may need some more convincing." She laughed as she ran her fingernails gently up the inside of his thigh.

He pulled away as he quickly responded, "I wish I could, but Diane is fixing dinner for me tonight, and I promised her I'd be on time. I'm really worried about her; she's just weeks from having the baby. I can't believe Sy would put her through this, that miserable bastard."

Sharon smiled. "You could come over to my place tomorrow. We don't need to be seen every time we go out. I would love some alone time with you."

Sammy leaned in, quietly saying, "I will if I can, but since I have so much going on, you can't hold me to it."

Sharon snapped, "Well, you'd better get to your daughter's house then; we don't want her upset."

Sammy shot up from the chair and headed to the valet window, leaving Sharon sitting there with a scowl on her face.

Sammy pulled up in front of Diane's house, a small but charming cottage located in an old upper-middle-class neighborhood that had become the lower-middle-class part of town. He walked up the steps to the front door and noticed for the first time how small it was and how close the other houses were. As he looked around, he noticed the houses all had the same front porches that appeared to be lined up on purpose. He thought, *I have to get her out of here and into a decent neighborhood.* He considered moving them into his new Brownstone townhomes in East Memphis—a much better neighborhood and a larger home for the new addition. Diane opened the door before he could knock. She wore a cute maternity top with an arrow pointing down that said "Baby on board." She welcomed him into their tiny living room furnished with only a sofa and chair. He chose the chair. Before he could sit, Michael greeted him with a warm handshake and smile and offered him a drink.

"No, I'm fine, thanks. So how are you two handling this horrible media circus?"

"I'm fine, except for the sickening news coverage on all the channels," Diane said. "I still can't believe Uncle Sy could do this to us."

"It's a pack of lies. I loved your mother. I'd never do anything to hurt her. You believe me, don't you?"

"Of course I believe you, Daddy."

35

RACHEL COULD FEEL HER BRUISED AND BEATEN HEART STARTING TO feel alive again. A smile crept over her face. For the first time in a long time, she felt she had a purpose. She was going to trial to get justice for her sister. Every day, she wanted to call the psychic to get answers to the many questions she still didn't understand. Darlene's words, "you cannot kill the soul," kept running through Rachel's mind. It was hard for her to wrap her head around the concept, even though it was, in essence, the same as the biblical teaching that people live for eternity. She was sure she had spoken to her sister through the psychic, so what other explanation could there be? Her soul must have survived her body. The way the psychic spoke softly, the inflections she used, and the mannerisms were all Hope's. The psychic had never met Hope, so how could she mimic her so perfectly? It couldn't be a hoax; nobody was that good.

Rachel knew she was betraying the promise she had made to Syrus, but she just had to talk to her sister again; she couldn't stop herself. She knew she should not call the psychic, and even as she was trying to talk herself out of calling, she was dialing Darlene's number.

"Hi, Darlene. I desperately need to talk to Hope again, but I'm afraid to come near your house. Syrus seems to think someone is watching every move we make, so I was wondering if there's any chance you could possibly come to my house to channel Hope?"

Darlene was gracious as always. "Certainly, I'd be happy to."

They settled on Monday morning.

As Rachel hung up, she breathed a sigh of relief and bowed her head, praying that Sy would never find out.

Over the weekend, she waited anxiously for their meeting. She was sure Darlene had read the newspaper and watched the news coverage on TV since their last meeting and she was smart enough to have filled in the blanks, or intuitive enough to have pieced it together for sure.

The following Monday, Rachel kept looking out the window for any sign of Darlene. She wished now she had told her nine o'clock instead of ten. When the back gate creaked, Rachel walked over to the kitchen window and spotted Darlene approaching the back door, wearing a poncho, a wide-brimmed hat, and sunglasses. She hid behind the door as she invited Darlene in; if someone was watching the house, she didn't want them to see her.

Rachel quickly closed the door as she welcomed Darlene into her home. "How have you been? Has anyone contacted you in relation to the trial?"

Darlene smiled as she gently touched Rachel's shoulder, attempting to alleviate her concern. "There's nothing to worry about; no one has contacted me. With all the news coverage, I've been able to keep up with what's been going on with Sy and the upcoming trial."

"Thank goodness! You know the only reason I haven't called is because Sy forbade me for fear of someone finding out, because he thinks it would affect the case. Please don't be offended, but we must keep this meeting secret. I'm so sorry, but my relationship with Sy is still on shaky ground, and I certainly don't want to do anything that would make him mad. He's already telling me this case will probably force him into an early retirement—unless he wins, of course."

"I understand completely. Not to worry; I wouldn't do anything that would hurt you, Sy, or the case. Your secret is safe with me."

"Thank you, thank you. You have no idea how much that means to me. Let's go into the den. Can I make you some tea or coffee?"

Rachel showed her to the den and talked to her from the kitchen, where she prepared tea and arranged a plate of cheese-filled crumb cake. "Will you be comfortable enough in there to contact Hope?"

"I can feel her presence already; she likes to hang out in this room with you."

As Rachel entered the den carrying the tea, she smiled. "This is the room where I usually do my meditation. I sit right there." She pointed to the lounge seat on the end of the sofa. Rachel took deep breaths, trying to rein in her soaring emotions, knowing she would soon get to speak with her sister. She was quick to set her cup of tea down, anxious to get started.

Darlene set her tea on a nearby table and pushed back into the chair and said, "Let's do our meditation." She closed her eyes and took deep breaths, and her head lowered as she appeared to slump.

Soon Darlene straightened and began to talk. It seemed Hope had been waiting for them, because she came through right away. Rachel asked her questions about the day she died. Then she told her Sy was taking Sammy and Alfie to court for her murder, but Hope didn't respond to Rachel about this. She just repeatedly said, "It was not my time to go. I miss you so much. I want to come back. Please help me."

Soon after Darlene came out of the trance and said, "Hope's anguish was so bad I asked Hope's angels to intervene and comfort her. When she's like that, I have to break the connection because we are not helping her."

Rachel began questioning herself aloud. "I was going through such highs and lows before Hope was murdered; I feel as though I could have been more help if I hadn't been so self-absorbed. I blamed it on feeling neglected by my husband. I hate myself for missing all the red flags, knowing I might have been able to save her."

"Rachel, you shouldn't blame yourself. I want you to understand that part of what you were feeling was a psychic awareness of what Sammy was planning. You are much more psychic than you know. If you develop that ability, it will help you in the future. Everyone has some psychic ability and can develop it further, but some people have a more open channel; they're just born more connected.

"You mean all those times I felt anxiety and panic, I was picking up on his feelings?"

"No, not every time, but I think it became more intense as he got closer to killing her, because he was getting more excited. A lot of family members say he or she felt that something was wrong before a loved one was killed, especially when that loved one was killed by someone they knew. You are always tuned in to the people you love and to the people you hate. There is a thin line between strong emotions, both positive and negative. A well-known woman came to me after she was killed by her husband and said she didn't know why everyone was making such a fuss over her death, because *she* didn't care; she was relieved to have gotten out of the emotional trap she was in because of the love/hate relationship she had with her former husband."

Darlene continued. "Hope had gotten past her emotional attachment to Sammy, but she was in total denial about his true character. If you've never known a psychopath, it's hard to recognize that they are truly diabolical and proud of it. Hope wanted to keep the Sammy she fell in love with. She remained loving and trusting. She really believed she was his best friend.

Rachel sighed. "Really, I don't know why Hope couldn't see it; everyone else could. So who was the woman who came to you?"

"These sessions are confidential; I was just using her as an example. I don't know why she came to me, as there was nothing I could do with the information, but it did give me insight into different reasons for a soul's reactions to murder."

Rachel pondered what Darlene had said about being psychic. "So all those days I was feeling desperate and afraid, I was really picking up on Sammy's vibes that he was excited about planning her murder?"

"Some of the time. Some days you were missing the kids and that part of your life when they were dependent on you, being needed as only a mother and a father can be."

"Yes, so Sy is not having an affair with another woman?"

"No, I'm not seeing anything like that. He is going through a change of life. Men do too you know; they just act more macho and try to cover it up, like a cat trying to cover up its feces, hoping no one will notice."

Rachel slumped over, interlocking her fingers, staring at the floor. "Well, I still feel like we've lost our connection. I don't know what happened, but I don't think he loves me anymore. You know, he didn't say a word to me about the investigation he was doing until right up to the day he needed my help. I was in so much anguish; it would have helped to know he was trying to do something to help me. I just don't get it."

Darlene cocked her head gently. "That's something only the two of you can figure out. There's no easy answer, but it is something you'll have to work on together. I don't believe all is lost, but you're going to need to stop trying to guess what's wrong and talk to each other. Maybe talk to your therapist about new or different ways to talk to each other. I'm sure there's a way, so find the solution. Your marriage is worth the effort it will take to save it. And after this is over, y'all really do need to go on a vacation together."

"From your lips to God's ears!"

Darlene chuckled as she stood up to leave. "Yes, I wish you every success."

36

SAM AND ALFIE FIDGETED IN THE WAITING ROOM OF WAYNE EMMONS'S law office. It was nearly an hour before Sue Ellen finally came out to get them. She had the same big hair and big earrings but now had a cocky, redneck, "don't mess with me" attitude in her demeanor. As she held the door open, she directed them to follow her and escorted them to the conference room. There she asked whether they would like water or coffee. Alfie struggled to pull out a chair. "Yes, do you have Perrier?"

The secretary glared with disdain. "No, we only have regular Memphis water here."

Alfie tossed a hand on his hip and demanded, "Well, is it at least cold?"

The secretary frowned. "Do you want water or not?"

With that, Sammy jumped in. "Yes, please bring both of us a glass of water, thank you." Sammy shot Alfie an icy glare as she left the room. As soon as the door closed, he turned to Alfie. "Enough with the prissy gay thing; you need to man up now. And stay manned up all the way through the trial if you want me to get you out of this."

Alfred quickly straightened up, smoothed his tie and crossed his arms in the manliest pose he could muster. "I'm sorry, Mr. Grossman;

163

Lockard quickly rose. "With the court's permission, Your Honor, we'd like to reserve our opening statement until the beginning of our proof."

Judge Maxfield motioned to the DA. "Mr. Ramsey, do you have any objections?"

"No, Your Honor."

"Well then, call your first witness."

Mr. Ramsey stood as he announced, "The state calls Shelby County Medical Examiner Dr. Roger Lewis."

The doctor moved forward and stood to take the oath with his right hand on the Bible before being seated.

Ramsey swung into action. "Doctor, did you examine the remains of Hope Grossman?

"Yes, I received a court order—"

Emmons sprang from his seat. "Objection, Your Honor. We'd like to pose an objection at this time ... out of the presence of the jury."

The judge nodded as he motioned for the clerk to remove the jury.

The four attorneys assembled in front of the judge. "All right, Mr. Emmons, what's your objection?"

"Your Honor, Tennessee statute states the first next of kin must authorize an autopsy. In this case, the rightful and legal next of kin is Mr. Grossman, who neither authorized the autopsy nor was even notified. Therefore, the autopsy was illegal, the results of which cannot be used in evidence."

The judge leaned forward. "Mr. Ramsey?"

Ramsey moved forward to answer. "Your Honor, the order was issued by Judge Davis. Whereby foul play was suspected involving the first next of kin, the deceased's mother could and did authorize the autopsy. The death certificate states she died from asphyxiation, but this witness will testify to the actual cause of death, which was cyanide poisoning. So, while it may have violated the letter of the law, it did not violate the *spirit of the law*, which is to determine Mrs. Grossman's actual cause of death."

Judge Maxfield leaned back in his chair, deep in thought, and then suddenly sat forward, pushing his glasses back on his nose, "Since Judge

Davis felt there were sufficient grounds to issue the order, I'm not going to disturb it at this time. Mr. Emmons, your objection is overruled."

Emmons turned on his heels and shot a dirty look at Sy while going back to his table. Soon after the clerk led the jury back into the courtroom.

Ramsey took a bracing breath and continued the questioning. "Dr. Lewis, based on a reasonable medical certainty, what is your opinion as to the cause of death?"

"Hope Grossman died of cyanide poisoning."

"How much cyanide was present in her body?"

"While I don't have an exact amount, I would guess it was more than the size of a capsule pill like Tylenol, which is more than any person could have survived."

Before Ramsey could even get back to the table, Emmons raced forward to begin his cross-examination.

"Dr. Lewis, you're not saying that you know how the poison got into Mrs. Grossman's body; you are just stating the fact that poison was found in her system, correct?"

"Yes, that's right."

"As the coroner of Shelby County for more than twenty years, have you handled many poisoning deaths?"

"Yes, I've seen a number of cases."

"How many of those were suicides?"

Syrus leaped to his feet. "Objection! No foundation, Your Honor. There's not the slightest suggestion or evidence of suicide here. He's trying to confuse the jury by putting in something that's not in evidence."

Judge Maxfield looked to Emmons. "Where are you going with this?"

"He's testifying as an expert on poisonings. I just wanted to ask, of the many cases he's handled, how many were suicides, homicides, and accidents."

"I'll allow that. Objection overruled."

Syrus sat back down, fuming, as Emmons continued. "Doctor, what percentage of the poisoning cases that you've investigated turned out to be suicides?"

"Probably twenty percent."

"How many were homicides?"

"About forty percent. The rest were accidental, as in children swallowing rat poison or drain cleaner."

"But Doctor, you can't actually determine whether it was suicide, homicide, or accidental just by examining the body, can you?"

"That's correct."

"No further questions, Your Honor."

Emmons took his seat, and Lockard stood up to face Dr. Lewis, the picture of smiling graciousness. "Dr. Lewis, would there be any difference in the appearance of a person that's died of asphyxiation and one that's died of cyanide poisoning?"

"Generally speaking, very little difference, though there could be vomit or foam in the mouth."

"So, Doctor, without an autopsy, there would be no other absolute way of determining the cause of death."

"That's right."

"So if the average person were eating with someone who started choking and gasping for breath, and died, that person would probably assume the person who died choked to death, wouldn't he?"

"Yes, he could."

"No more questions, Your Honor."

As Dr. Lewis left the stand, Ramsey called the next witness. "Mr. William Bryan Gillpatrick. Mr. Gillpatrick, are you a vice president at Memphis Bank & Trust?"

"Yes."

"Mr. Gillpatrick, did your bank make a loan to Mr. Grossman and his partner, Mr. Birmingham, for real estate referred to as the Brownstone Project?"

"Yes, we did."

"What was the amount of the loan?"

"Five million, six hundred thousand dollars."

"How was the loan secured?"

"By a trust deed against the property itself, and second trust deeds on the personal homes of Mr. and Mrs. Grossman and Mr. Birmingham."

"Had the bank begun foreclosure on the note before Mrs. Grossman's death?"

"Yes."

"And what would have happened if the bank had foreclosed?"

"They would have forfeited all properties used to secure the loan."

"How soon after Hope Grossman's death were the payments brought up to date?"

"Within forty days."

"Thank you, Mr. Gillpatrick. No more questions, Your Honor."

Emmons quickly announced, "We have no questions of this witness, Your Honor."

The judge called for a fifteen-minute break, and when they returned, Ramsey called Mr. Dan Tanasijevic to the stand and began questioning him.

"Mr. Tanasijevic, did you sell a million-dollar double indemnity life insurance policy to Mr. and Mrs. Samuel Grossman?"

"Yes."

"I have a document from General Life Insurance stating the insurance was purchased February 11, 1991. Is that correct?"

"Yes."

"Mr. Tanasijevic, did your insurance company do an investigation before paying Mr. Grossman?"

"Yes, one of our best investigators was immediately sent to the Bahamas to question the authorities and examine their records."

"But your company paid out two million dollars on an accidental death without an autopsy. Is that normal?"

"No, but in this case we felt the investigation was thorough and there was no reason to go against our client's religious beliefs. Our customer always comes first, and we try to honor our client's requests if possible."

"Yes, and did you feel the same way after you found your client had defrauded the company?"

Emmons shot up from his chair. "Objection! Objection, Your Honor!"

The judge gave him a grim grin. "Sustained."

171

Mr. Tanasijevic, when were you contacted and told the death of Hope Grossman was not an accident?"

"Mr. Grossman's attorney contacted me shortly before it was announced on the news."

"And what was your corporation's response to the information?"

"It is handled by our corporate offices and I am not privy to that information"

Ramsey grinned as he replied, "No more questions, Your Honor."

Emmons declined to question the witness.

The judge announced, "We're going to stop for today; be back here tomorrow morning at 9:00 a.m."

38

THE NEXT MORNING, RAMSEY, SY, AND RACHEL ALL ENTERED THE courthouse from the back alley so as not to be accosted by the media. Sy had Rachel stay in a private office until she was called to the stand.

Ramsey and Sy were the first ones in the courtroom. As soon as everyone was assembled, the court was called to order. Soon after, Bryan Ramsey stood and made the announcement, "The state calls Rachel Marcus."

All heads turned and watched as the double doors opened and Rachel walked down the aisle to the witness stand. Syrus turned and smiled as he looked, with adoring eyes, at his wife. She was dressed in an all-white suit and a white satin blouse with a ruffled lace collar as she moved gracefully down the aisle. Sparkling rhinestone clips swept her hair back and held it in place on either side. The sun shining through the windows beaming off the rhinestone hair clips gave the appearance of an aureole around her head. She was somber as she took the oath. As Ramsey began questioning her, she looked at the jury and smiled.

"What was your relationship to the deceased?"

"She was my sister."

"Would you consider yourself close?"

People gasped and whispered. Some of the reporters scrambled to get outside to phones while the judge banged his gavel. "Order! order!"

Rachel looked defiantly at Sammy who looked back with scorn, while Alfie, red-faced and livid, mouthed, "You bitch."

Emmons stood and stepped forward. "Your Honor, giving an opinion is not admissible. We'd like that last remark stricken from the record and the jury admonished to disregard it."

"Objection sustained. The jury will please disregard that last remark." The judge motioned to Ramsey. "You may continue, Mr. Ramsey."

"Mrs. Marcus, from your personal knowledge of the Grossman marriage, did any of their problems involve Alfred Birmingham?"

"Yes. Whenever I was at their home, Alfie was always there. He followed Sammy around like a lap dog, obeying his every command. He never left them alone."

"Tell us what you observed after your sister's death."

Rachel straightened and took a deep breath as she turned to face the jury. "Sammy moved in with Alfie. They were inseparable. Sammy did not get his own place until after he was arrested. They work together, they travel together, and I'm sure they sleep together."

There were gasps, whispers, and reactions in the courtroom. By now Emmons was fuming, stomping as he stood. Sarcastically he quipped, "Objection to the gratuitous comments and conclusions of the witness. Please admonish her to stay with the facts rather than these ludicrous opinions."

Ramsey shot back, "Your Honor, again, these accounts are of her own knowledge that go to the motive for the murder."

"Objection sustained. Please limit your answers to the questions asked."

Rachel nodded politely to the judge.

"Was there any time Hope and Sammy were separated or started divorce proceedings?"

"Yes. After that incident, Hope and Sammy slept in separate bedrooms. Hope was convinced Sammy and Alfie were lovers, so she took an HIV test."

"How do you know that?"

"I drove her to get the test."

"Did anyone else know about their marital problems?"

"Yes, a close friend of ours—an attorney, Louis Berger. She met with him about filing for divorce. He advised Hope to wait until the brownstones were completed so she would have something to bargain with; otherwise, she'd have nothing except the inheritance she got from our father. Everything was tied up in the Brownstones. I don't think she had any idea they were in that much financial trouble, or she would have told me. I even asked her once if Sammy had asked her to give him the money from her inheritance, and she said he hadn't ever brought up the subject. Of course not, because his name was on the account in case of death. I told her back then that if they needed help, Sy and I would loan them some money."

Ramsey gave Rachel a sly smile before turning toward the defense lawyers' table. "Thank you. Your witness."

Emmons leapt from his chair and charged toward Rachel. She remained poised and defiant.

"Mrs. Marcus, you said your sister did not file for divorce. Did she tell Sammy she had talked to Mr. Berger?"

"She told him."

"And what was his reaction?"

Syrus stood and bellowed out, "Objection, Your Honor—hearsay!"

The judge nodded. "Sustained."

Mr. Emmons continued. "Mr. Grossman got an HIV test, didn't he?"

Rachel flicked imaginary lint from her sleeve. "That's what I heard."

"Yes or no?"

Ramsey stood. "Objection, objection. Once again, hearsay, Your Honor."

"Sustained."

"They started seeing a marriage counselor together, didn't they?"

"Yes."

"Didn't things get better between them?"

"It appeared they did."

"Hadn't your sister just gone through surgery for breast cancer and then months of chemotherapy?"

"Yes, she did."

"And how did Sammy treat Hope during her surgery and the recovery?"

Rachel glanced over at Sammy, who was watching the jury. "He appeared genuinely concerned."

"Did he appear distressed or repulsed by her disfigurement?"

"Not in front of me."

"Didn't he bring her flowers often and stay with her as much as possible during her hospitalization?"

"Yes."

Didn't he hire a psychologist after the surgery to help her cope?"

"Yes."

"Does this sound like a man who wanted to murder his wife?"

"No, but—"

"No! It sounds like a man trying to save his marriage and help his wife want to live. Doesn't it, Mrs. Marcus?"

"Sure; he'd get twice as much money if she died from an accident than from cancer."

Emmons frowned as he rushed into the next question. "Mrs. Marcus, wasn't the real reason your sister didn't want a divorce because she still loved Sammy and thought they could work things out?"

"No, she was biding her time until the brownstones were finished and generating an income."

"Your Honor …"

"Then she planned to divorce him."

Judge Maxfield sighed. "Mrs. Marcus, again, you must confine your answers to the questions asked. The jury will disregard that last comment, and it will be stricken from the record."

"Isn't it true that it was your idea that Hope get the HIV test?"

"After she told me her suspicions, I encouraged her to get it for her peace of mind."

"And didn't you introduce her to your friend Mr. Berger?"

"She's known him for years; he's always been a part of our social group, and she needed a good divorce attorney. She was miserable."

"You've testified that Hope was your only sister and that the two of you were very close; am I correct?"

"Yes."

"Sammy didn't have a brother, did he?"

"No, he has sisters."

"So when a man doesn't have a close relationship with a brother, he may still want a close male friend, right?"

Rachel nonchalantly straightened her lace collar. "I suppose."

"If these two were passionately in love, as you would like us to believe, wouldn't someone besides you be able to testify to that fact?"

"If it looks like a duck, walks like a duck, *and* quacks like a duck ..."

A ripple of laughter ran through the courtroom.

Emmons looked at the judge sharply and raised his hands in disgust.

The judge gave Rachel a stern look. "Mrs. Marcus, just answer the question with a simple yes or no."

Emmons paused dramatically, took a deep breath, and paced. "I'll rephrase the question. You've never seen them kiss or hold hands, never seen any photos, and you've never seen them in bed together, have you?" He whirled around and moved in as he lashed out at her. "Yet you decided they're homosexual lovers?"

"I've seen Alfie's jealous rages; what about those?"

"I would like an answer to the question. Have you ever seen them in bed together?"

"No."

"Have you ever seen them kiss or hold hands?"

"No."

"Isn't it possible that Alfred was envious of the relationship between Hope and Sammy? That he might never know the joy of love between a man and a woman, of having children, or of being accepted by society? Isn't that possible?"

"Possible, but highly improbable."

Emmons looked to the jury and then to the audience. "When two men work and travel together, does that automatically mean they're gay?"

"No."

"In fact, a man in the company of men is commonplace and revered in many cultures, such as a man named Jesus who traveled all over the Holy Land in the company of twelve men. No one suggested they were homosexuals ... Well, strike that; a few, devious, small-minded persons such as yourself have suggested that, have they not?"

Syrus leapt to his feet. "Objection, Your Honor! Badgering the witness. Mr. Emmons is completely out of line."

"Objection sustained."

"No more questions, Your Honor."

Ramsey stood up, "Your Honor, we'd like to request that Rachel Marcus be held as a recall witness."

"Request granted. We are going to break early today for the Thanksgiving holiday. We will reconvene Monday morning at 9:00 a.m."

39

RACHEL WAS VERY HAPPY AT THE WAY THE TRIAL WAS GOING. SHE HAD planted the seed that Sammy and Alfie were gay, something she and Hope had talked about in the last year. To Rachel, the only other explanation would be if Sammy were so diabolical that he would pretend to be gay to manipulate Alfie to get rid of Hope. None of it made any sense to her. For a long time, there had been a complex blend of love and loathing in Hope and Sammy's relationship, so how and when had it turned into nothing but loathing? It was beyond Rachel's grasp to understand how Sammy could justify killing Hope for any reason. And Alfie—how could he go along with it? Or was he the psycho? Did he plot her demise so he could have Sammy all to himself? Was he so in love that he would be willing to take the risk of losing Sammy forever if he were caught?

Rachel was glad to go back to her shop, where she could pretend this was all happening in another life. Almost no one asked her about the trial. She had made it crystal clear in every conversation that she was not allowed to talk about it legally or personally; thank goodness her clients respected that.

She was in her shop early the Saturday after Thanksgiving, as there was a lot to do to prepare for the upcoming party season.

Rachel had just unlocked the front door and was putting the finishing touches on a mannequin when Diane came bursting through the door. Diane was trembling and on the verge of tears when she confronted her. "Aunt Rachel, what's going on with you?"

Rachel tried to take Diane's arm to lead her back to her office, but she furiously pulled away and started shouting at Rachel.

"Have you seen the TV? It's outrageous what they're saying about Daddy. He would never hurt Mom. He loved her."

Rachel spoke sweetly, "This must be awful for you …"

"How could you say those things in court? How could you do this to our family?"

"I'm sorry, Diane. I've been hoping to talk with you about this; I just didn't know what I could say that would make it any easier."

"Did Uncle Sy tell you what he was going to do?"

"We discussed it, but—"

"How could you let him do this to our family? It's crazy and it's a lie!"

"Sy thinks—"

"Can't you stop him?"

Rachel placed her hands gently on Diane's shoulders and looked into her eyes. "Please listen to me, Diane. You're going to find out anyway. I asked Sy to do this. It was my idea."

Diane stepped back sharply as though she'd been slapped. "What? But that's insane. Daddy didn't have anything to do with Momma's death; he couldn't have."

"We have proof he—"

"What proof? It had to be Alfie. He's always acted jealous of Mom. He was the one with her."

"We believe they planned it together."

"Are you crazy? Daddy loved Mom. He had no reason to kill her."

"He collected over two million dollars in life insurance."

"So what? That doesn't prove anything!" Tears poured down Diane's cheeks. "How could you do this to me? Mom would hate you for doing this!"

Rachel, gently cupping Diane's face in her hands, spoke to her as sympathetic as she could, trying to come up with some way of telling her that made sense. "I love you so much, and there's so much more to tell you about your mother's death. I will tell you everything, but please calm down. It's not good for you or the baby."

Diane took Rachel's hands from her face and cried out indignantly, "How dare you act like you care about me or my baby ... you ..." Diane gasped as she grabbed her belly.

Rachel grabbed hold of her. "Are you all right?"

Diane pulled from her grip and started for the bathroom. "Leave me alone."

Diane stopped and held on to the counter as she cried out in pain. "Oh God, I think my water broke."

"I'll take you to the hospital; we can call the doctor on the way. You'll be fine, Diane, I'll—"

"Stay away from me; I'm calling Michael." She reached for the phone on the desk and started dialing.

Diane cried quietly while waiting for Michael. Rachel tried to help her to the car when Michael arrived, but she pushed her away. As Michael helped Diane into the car, Rachel said, "I'll meet you at the hospital." Michael replied through clenched teeth, "Don't you dare come to the hospital; we don't want anything to do with you."

Rachel watched the car drive off. Tears streaked her face as the feeling of loss returned in full force—that empty, vile feeling that once again events had taken a precious piece of her life.

Rachel went to the desk and called her assistant and asked her to get to the shop immediately because she had an emergency. As soon as Belle arrived, Rachel left for the hospital. When she got there, she rushed to the nurse's station near the delivery rooms. "My niece, Diane Katz, is in labor. Can you tell me if she is okay? Are they delivering the baby?"

The nurse politely replied, "I'll go see what I can find out."

Soon after, Michael emerged from behind the doors of the delivery rooms, seething and prepared for battle.

"Is she okay?"

"She's fine. She doesn't want to see you, and she doesn't want you here."

"Please tell her I love her very much and I'll be here if she needs me."

Michael's face was red, and his fists were clenched. "You've already done enough. The baby is coming early because of what you've done to her. Do us all a favor; get out of our lives and stay out." Michael abruptly turned his back on Rachel and slammed through the doors, muttering profanities.

Rachel wiped away the tears welling up from inside. There was so much she wanted to tell Diane, including that she had been talking to her mother through a psychic and that her mother was in terrible anguish and needed Rachel's help. But how could she explain that to her now? If only Diane knew what she knew, Rachel surmised, she would understand and forgive her.

Rachel made her way out to her car while trying to maintain a semblance of composure. As soon as she was in the privacy of her car, however, she dissolved into tears and began trembling so much that she could barely pick up the phone. She put the phone back and wept until she couldn't cry anymore. Once she felt in control, she took a deep breath, wiped her face, and had a stern talk with herself. She knew she had to pull herself together before calling Belle, but when she did call, Belle immediately could sense something was terribly wrong. "Rachel, what happened? Is your niece okay?"

"Yes. She went into labor, and I'm at the hospital. The baby is coming early, and that's not good, so I'm staying here until the baby is delivered. I won't be back today, so please take care of my appointments and let my clients know that I won't be available today and probably not on Monday either. I can't leave Diane alone at a time like this. I'll call you on Monday morning. Thanks again. Bye." Rachel wished she didn't have to lie, but she couldn't tell her assistant the truth, either. *My life is a disaster, and all because Sammy is tangled up with Alfie.* Rachel had always thought Sammy was narcissistic, and she wondered if he had ever thought about how this would affect all the other people in his life: his own daughter, her, Mom, Sy, and all of the other family members on both sides. *When did he decide to become a killer? Is it really all about the money, or is he hiding his sexuality?* There were so many family members with the money to help him; how could he possibly believe that murder was the solution?

She was distraught, and even though she knew she should not, she desperately wanted to talk with her sister. She picked up the car phone and dialed Darlene. A stranger answered the phone and told her to hold on and she would get her.

"Hi, Rachel."

Rachel's voice, though restrained, was audibly emotional. "Darlene, I really need to talk to my sister; her daughter is so angry with me I don't know what to do. Could you see me today?"

"I'm so sorry, but my daughter and her family are here for the weekend and I can't see you before Monday."

"What time on Monday?"

"In the afternoon. How is four thirty for you?"

"That's fine."

"Do you want me to come to your house?"

"Oh no, the media is stalking us now, including the house."

"Then come to my house and drive to the back alley; no one will see you. I'll have the garage door open for you. You can pull in there, and we can close the garage door."

"That's good. I'll see you then. Thank you."

Rachel stayed in the hospital parking lot for a while; she didn't know what to do. She thought about calling Sy but decided to go to her mother's instead and tell her the news about Diane and the baby. Her mother could call the hospital to see how they were doing. She thought maybe Sara could talk to Diane to smooth things over for her.

When Rachel arrived at her mother's and told her what had happened, her mother called the hospital to see if everything was okay. All they would tell her was that Diane was still in labor.

Later, when she arrived home, Sy and their kids were in the family room. She greeted them, but no one other than Mindy paid her any attention. Sy and Jason were engrossed in a college football game on TV. Rachel told them she would start dinner and went into the kitchen.

The TV was in a built-in wall unit with the sofa directly opposite, for perfect viewing. Sy lay on the lounge end of the rustic red sectional sofa. Jason was sitting at the other end. Mindy was in the adjacent swivel chair, pretending interest in the game.

When the ads came on, Jason started asking questions. "Dad, why is there so much media attention in this case? Is it because you're related to Uncle Sam?"

"No, it's more than that. It's because Sammy is a prominent businessman and his business partner is gay. But most of all, it's because the media was barred from the courtroom. This judge hates the media; he calls them the devil's toolbox. The media hates being barred from the courtroom, but of course that does not stop them from twisting the information any way they want. God forbid they rely on the facts."

"You mean they can say things that aren't in the record."

"Yes, son. Does that surprise you? I hope you kids understand this is just another trial like all the others. This one has just garnered more attention than it should. Don't buy into all the crap, okay?"

Mindy chimed in. "Okay, but Dad, we've had some pretty weird phone calls. I think Mom's scared. Why aren't you sleeping in your room with her?"

"It's nothing, kids; we're having some issues—things that every couple has from time to time. We are both stressed to the max between your aunt's death and Uncle Sammy being on trial for her murder. It'll be over soon, and things will get back to normal."

Jason was still thinking about the trial as he said, "Dad, I really wish I could be in the courtroom with you next week. I'm thinking about going into law. It's never boring, I could make good money, and I could learn from the best—you."

Sy smiled broadly. "You sure could, son. Come to court; I'll get you a front-row seat."

"I would if it weren't for my semester finals starting next week; I can't miss those."

"No, you can't miss those, but there will be plenty of other trials later that you can experience with me. You could work in my law offices next summer if you wanted."

"That would be great, Dad!"

Rachel listened to the family talking as she prepared dinner. She wished she could tell Sy what had happened at the hospital, but she could sense he was not in the mood. Rachel knew he would blame her, and then he'd say, "What did you expect?"

When dinner was ready, she called for the kids, and they ate their dinner at the kitchen table with her. Sy had gone into his office and did not come out when she called him, so she took his dinner in to him, but he wouldn't even look at her. He mumbled his thanks as he continued reading the document in his hand.

The kids were anxious to go out with their friends, so Rachel gave them some money, and they left. She walked down the hall toward Sy's office, but his door was closed, and that meant he did not want to be disturbed. She slumped over as she plodded up the stairs to her bedroom, got ready for bed, took a Valium, and crawled under the blankets. She turned on the TV to escape from any further thoughts of the day's events. The local news covered the latest criminal being arrested. The story caught her attention because they were talking about Buford Hollis, the same criminal Sy had gotten off for murder. He had raped another little girl and was attempting to strangle her when someone saw them in the back alley and stopped him. Thankfully the little girl had lived to tell about it. When the phone rang, it frightened her; it was so late it could be only the kids or one of Sy's clients. She picked it up and heard Sy say, "Hello."

She wanted to know if the kids were calling or if the call had something to do with them, but then she heard a voice say, "Syrus, my man, it's Buford Hollis. I'm in jail, but I've got fifty thousand dollars says you can get me outta here. You gotta help me, Syrus; this is my only phone call, so you need to call the bondsman for me."

"What are you charged with?"

"Attempted murder and rape, because they say they saw me in the alley with that girl. I didn't do nothin'. I'm innocent."

"How old is the girl?"

"I don't know … maybe eighteen or nineteen. She was working the streets. I paid her for her services; it wasn't rape."

"Was there something in particular that made them suspicious enough to order an autopsy?"

Staring off into space, Sara went into her own world of memories. "They had such beautiful hair. When they were little, I would braid Rachel's hair while she braided Hope's."

"Did Rachel talk to a woman named Darlene Evans?"

"I don't know; she may have. Sara smiled sweetly, leaning in to him. "So are you married? A man your age should have a wife."

"I guess you could say I haven't found the right one."

"For a man like you, I know many nice girls … More cake?"

"Maybe just a little. It's delicious; reminds me of my mother's cooking."

"You're Jewish?"

"No, but a lot of my friends are. Sara, do you know how Rachel knew about the insurance policy?"

"You should talk to my son-in-law, Syrus; he knows all about this."

Sara looked at Heller's plate with the uneaten cake on it. "You don't like the cake? I have some nice strudel in the freezer. Let me warm you a piece."

Heller held up both hands in surrender. "That's so nice of you, but I have to get back to the office; I have a deadline to meet to get this into tomorrow's paper. Thanks again for meeting with me; you've been very helpful."

41

THE NEXT MORNING, AS SYRUS ROUNDED THE CORNER HEADING FOR the courthouse, he was surprised to see lots of people on the streets and crowding on the courthouse steps. He could read some of the signs easily; they were obviously homemade. Some read, "Fry the Fags" and "Psychics =Devil's Workshop." A group of skinheads carried a sign reading, "Long live the Klan," and one particularly vocal woman waved a sign that read, "God is on our side."

As Syrus approached the crowd, some cheered him as others booed him. He politely pushed his way through the crowd and hurried into the building. As he headed down the hallway to the courtroom, he saw Ramsey waving him into an office. He followed him into the room. "What in the hell is going on?"

Ramsey angrily waved a newspaper that was turned to the opinion page. He read the short take article aloud. "'What is our legal system coming to when it allows a hot shot defense attorney with a personal vendetta to waste the taxpayer's money? Syrus Marcus got himself appointed special prosecutor so he could go after his own brother-in-law. What type of persuasion did Marcus use to get our overworked DA to participate in this travesty, particularly when it's a case of flimsy circumstantial evidence laced with bigotry and trips to a psychic? Perhaps Mr. Marcus is allowing his personal bias to cloud his judgment.'" Ramsey glared at him. "Do you want to hear more?"

"Damn, who wrote that?"

"Don Heller, obviously not one of your biggest fans. Why is he out to get you? And how in the hell did he find out about the psychic? I thought no one knew but you, me, and Rachel."

"No one else does know… except the psychic."

"I thought you said she could be trusted. I'm not going to watch my career go down the toilet because of some crazy psychic!"

Sy ran a frustrated hand through his hair. "Okay, we've got to get to the courtroom right now, but I'll call Rachel when we have a break."

Ramsey opened the door to leave and curtly said, "Yeah, just make sure it's a private call."

The courtroom was packed and noisy. Ramsey and Marcus took their place, and Syrus whispered to Marty, soon after he left the courtroom.

Lockard walked to Emmons's side of the table to speak privately to him. "Did you see Heller's piece in the paper?" Emmons nodded. "It's priceless. The subject of psychics always incites the religious right, but maybe the witches will have a new hero."

Emmons said, "Yeah, I just feel bad for the KKK. With a black man and a Jew prosecuting gays, they won't know who to cheer for." Emmons and Lockard were jubilant over the scathing editorial. Both men were smiling as the judge came in and the court was called to order.

Syrus called his next witness, Lawrence Turner.

"Mr. Turner, how do you know the defendant, Samuel Grossman?"

"I was the estate attorney who executed wills for him and his wife."

"In an estate that size, the attorney who wrote the will would be the logical choice for Mr. Grossman's executor. Were you?"

"That information would be considered privileged."

"Well, I believe your client, Mr. Grossman, wouldn't want to hide the contents of his will from the jury … Syrus turned and vigorously directed his questioning to Sammy. I'm sure he'd want to waive the privilege—wouldn't you, Mr. Grossman?"

All eyes were on Sammy as he conferred with his lawyer. Syrus took his chance as he bellowed out to Sammy, "Isn't the executor your lover, Alfred Birmingham?"

The audience gasped, and there were a few boos and cheers as Emmons leapt to his feet. "Objection! Instruct counsel not to comment further until we approach the bench."

Syrus turned to the jury and looked them in the eyes. "I withdraw the question."

Judge Maxfield immediately turned to the jury, pronouncing loudly, "Objection sustained. The jury is to disregard that last question, and it's to be stricken from the record. And a warning to the spectators: any further outbursts in my courtroom, and you will be removed! Mr. Marcus, continue."

"No more questions, Your Honor."

Emmons quickly stood. "We have no questions for this witness, Your Honor."

"All right, call your next witness."

"The state calls Sharon Chambliss."

Sharon walked down the aisle in stiletto heels and a hot-pink suit. The skirt was short, and the jacket had a cheap knock-off Chanel flower on the lapel. She wiggled and smiled as she took the oath and then made eye contact with every man on the jury.

"Ms. Chambliss, were you on the yacht at the time of Hope Grossman's death?" Syrus asked.

"Yes."

"Did you poison Hope Grossman?"

Sharon's eyes went theatrically wide. "Why no! She is one of my oldest and dearest friends."

"We have an eyewitness who saw you and Sammy kissing and acting intimate at the Hotel Peabody bar. What exactly is your relationship with Sammy?"

"That's just since Hope died."

"So are you now having an intimate relationship with Sammy?"

"No, we're good friends who were just comforting each other."

"Have you had sex with Sammy?"

"No."

"Have you ever been to a party at Alfred's house?"

"No."

"Do you have any firsthand knowledge of intimate relations between Alfred and Sammy?"

"No, but I know Sammy's not gay, if that's what you're getting at."

"How could you know if you've never had sex with him?"

"Well, just having sex with a man wouldn't tell you anyway. Why, there are lots of men and women who are bisexual."

"Are you bisexual?"

"Now that's none of your business."

Emmons stood. "Objection, Your Honor. This line of questioning has no relevance in this case."

"Sustained; let's move on, Mr. Marcus."

Sy nodded as he proceeded. "So your opinion of Sammy is based on knowing him through Hope; is that right?"

"Yes."

"Did Hope ever say anything to you about their sex life or express fears of Sammy being gay?"

"Lord, no. Miss Goody Two-shoes wouldn't talk about sex—not even with Sammy."

"How do you know that?"

"Oh, well, I don't know; I'm just going by how Hope was."

"You must have a reason for knowing that, what—

Emmons, obviously irritated, said loudly, "Objection, Your Honor. Again there is no relevance to this line of questioning."

"Sustained; let's move on, Mr. Marcus."

"Do you now or have you ever worked for Samuel Grossman?"

"Yes. I'm a real estate agent, and I am working with Sammy to sell townhomes at his brownstone property."

"Were you working with Sammy before Hope's death?"

"Yes."

"So you spent a lot of time with Sammy before and after Hope's death, but you want us to believe you're nothing but friends."

Emmons stood. "Objection, Your Honor. Again this has no relevance in this case."

"Objection sustained."

"No more questions, Your Honor."

The judge turned to Emmons and Lockard. "Mr. Emmons? Mr. Lockard?"

"We have no questions, but we do want her on our list as a recall witness, Your Honor."

Syrus sat back down, and Ramsey stood. "We have no further witnesses. The state rests, Your Honor."

"It's late, gentlemen. We'll begin tomorrow with the defense's opening statement."

Ramsey and Marcus parted in the hallway, and Marcus headed for the back door, trying to avoid the crowd. Two attorneys hailed him. "Hey, Marcus, what'd your horoscope say this morning—that you were going to have a shitty day?"

The other attorney chimed in. "Yeah, you should try something a little more reliable next time … like a Ouija board!"

They laughed heartily at their own wit. Syrus remained impassive; he would not give them the satisfaction of a reaction. He needed to get home and find out how the news media had dug up the information about the psychic. His greatest fear had come true. The psychic had found a way to profit off the knowledge she had, and had betrayed him, as well as Rachel.

42

THE NEXT MORNING, THE CROWD HAD MUSHROOMED TO INCLUDE more protestors with signs and a bigger media presence. When Bryan and Syrus approached the courthouse and saw the crowd they went to the side of the building and around to the back entrance. The courtroom was packed, and many more bystanders were in the hall, hoping for a chance to get inside. Syrus and Bryan presented their bravest demeanor as they took their place in the courtroom. As soon as the spectators were seated and the doors closed, the judge appeared and court was called to order. Emmons swaggered to the front of the jury to deliver his opening statement, oozing with good-ol'-boy charm. He was smooth and articulate as he commanded their attention.

"Ladies and gentlemen of the jury, it's been established that Hope Grossman died from cyanide. That fact is not in dispute. But the defense will show that these men could not possibly have killed her, because Hope Grossman committed suicide."

A murmur ran through the audience as the judge pounded his gavel. "Order! Order, please!"

Emmons boldly moved in closer to the jury and proclaimed, "And we have her authenticated suicide note to prove it."

Emmons picked up a letter encased in plastic, and the courtroom again went wild. Syrus and Ramsey both jumped to their feet.

Ramsey and Syrus simultaneously declared, "Objection, Your Honor; may we approach the bench?"

Judge Maxfield growled, "I'd like counsel in my chambers, now! There'll be a ten-minute recess."

Moments later, the judge was examining the suicide note. Syrus was outraged as he read the note.

"It isn't even signed!"

"Your Honor, we have sworn statements from two graphologists and her own daughter saying the handwriting in this note belonged to the deceased."

Sy defiantly said, "It's a piece of a note, and it's not even dated. Where did they dig this up, and why weren't we given this information beforehand?"

Emmons, acting concerned and compassionate, continued his argument. "Mr. Grossman wanted to spare his daughter and the family, if at all possible. If we had gotten a directed verdict, it would have never been revealed publicly."

Syrus was livid. "So now you want to smear Hope and put the victim on trial."

"My client has the right to defend himself against these serious charges … even if it means revealing something very unpleasant about the deceased."

Judge Maxfield took in a deep breath as he hung his head low, rubbing his forehead. When he looked up, he grimaced as he said, "I'm going to allow it to show state of mind, but the jury will be apprised that it isn't dated or signed."

Syrus turned on his heels and slammed through the door. Ramsey followed.

A short time later, they were back in court. Emmons waved the plastic-encased note with renewed enthusiasm. He leaned toward the jurors as he ranted, "This sealed note was found on the boat by Alfred Birmingham after Mrs. Grossman died. He gave it to the defendant when he arrived back in Memphis. It reads, 'Dear Sammy, I know this

43

Sharon was still livid that evening as she hammered on the door of Sammy's townhouse. Sammy opened the door, grabbed her arm, forcefully pulled her inside, and quickly shut the door. "What are you doing here?"

"You arrogant ass, no wonder you were so anxious for me to go on that trip with Hope. You were setting me up. You planned it all along, didn't you?"

Sammy grabbed her by the throat with one hand and fiercely picked her up and slammed her into the wall. "If I were you, Sharon, I'd keep my mouth shut and do exactly as I was told!"

As he let go of her throat, she coughed and gasped, but as soon as she caught her breath, she fired back at him. "You should never try to fuck me over! I'm the one who could tell them about Alfie—and all the rest of it, for that matter!"

"Tell them what? That sex is my hobby and Alfie is one of my toys?"

Sharon moved away from Sammy. "I can tell them a lot more than that! How many times have you told me I need to learn to give head as good as Alfie does? Why don't I tell them that?"

Sammy grinned. "Yes, why don't you tell them, and I'll tell them

I have the taped conversation where you said, 'Let's kill Hope; we can use cyanide.' If you say one word to anyone, I'll see to it the DA's office gets it!"

Sharon shrieked. "You low-life bastard! I never said anything of the kind. I'm not going to prison for you."

"Well, let me play the tape; the only thing on it is your reference to killing Hope. I was the one who said, 'No, I could never do that.' Now, who do you think they're going to believe—me, the grieving husband, or you, the town's whore?"

Sharon raised her hand to hit him. Sammy quickly caught her arm in midair and twisted it behind her back as he pushed her into the wall, his voice chillingly savage as he spoke. "Listen to me, you piece of shit. You're going to keep your mouth shut. And don't ever show your face at my door again. And by the way, you're fired!" He thrust her arm higher as he pushed her toward the door, opened it, and shoved her out.

She gave him a look of absolute hatred as she hurled her threat at him. "You fucking maniac, you've just made the biggest mistake of your life!"

I was more financially stable because we needed to pay down the debt we had accrued with our real estate ventures."

"When did you move out of your home with Hope?"

"After I put my house up for sale, I had one of the brownstones custom finished for me. In September, when we returned from our last business trip, it was completed and ready to move into, which I did."

In the background, Ramsey and Marcus were quietly making notes and whispering to each other.

"You mentioned a trip. Why have you and Mr. Birmingham traveled together so often?"

"We're importers. Our trips are business related, and Hope came along at least half the time. She was always welcome to join me."

"When Hope didn't go with you, did you call home regularly?"

"Yes, I made frequent calls to my wife and daughter. They always knew where I was and how to reach me. My daughter can confirm that if you'd like to ask her."

"No, that's not necessary. Tell us how your wife felt about your relationship with Alfred."

"Alfie and Hope were close friends." Sammy paused and then turned to the jury and with emphasis said, "Until Rachel tried to convince her we were lovers."

"Were Hope and Alfred still close at the time of her death?"

"Yes. He helped me plan her birthday party and was as concerned about her welfare as I was. That is why he wanted her to join him the first week of the vacation. We had to board the yacht because we had reserved it. Otherwise, we would have lost the use of it for weeks. I couldn't leave, so Alfred went and had Hope join him so she could get some much-needed rest before I arrived." Sammy began to tear up. "If only I had been there, maybe she would still be alive." Sammy covered his face to hide his tears.

"Yes, Sam, why didn't you go the first week?"

"When Mr. Morgan offered me the use of the corporate yacht, he offered it for two weeks. I didn't think about it; I just said yes. Then, when it was closer to the time to go, I could only close the warehouse and office for one week. I paid vacation pay to my employees for the

I have the taped conversation where you said, 'Let's kill Hope; we can use cyanide.' If you say one word to anyone, I'll see to it the DA's office gets it!"

Sharon shrieked. "You low-life bastard! I never said anything of the kind. I'm not going to prison for you."

"Well, let me play the tape; the only thing on it is your reference to killing Hope. I was the one who said, 'No, I could never do that.' Now, who do you think they're going to believe—me, the grieving husband, or you, the town's whore?"

Sharon raised her hand to hit him. Sammy quickly caught her arm in midair and twisted it behind her back as he pushed her into the wall, his voice chillingly savage as he spoke. "Listen to me, you piece of shit. You're going to keep your mouth shut. And don't ever show your face at my door again. And by the way, you're fired!" He thrust her arm higher as he pushed her toward the door, opened it, and shoved her out.

She gave him a look of absolute hatred as she hurled her threat at him. "You fucking maniac, you've just made the biggest mistake of your life!"

44

SARA AND HER SISTER, DOROTHY, ATTENDED THE TRIAL EVERY DAY. They had to push through the protesters outside the courtroom, and were frightened by the hatred and ugliness they witnessed. Sara was also surprised to see a CNN van, as well as other news vans she didn't recognize. In addition, a bus with license plates from Louisiana had brought more demonstrators. She knew Syrus was a well-known lawyer, but she was confused as to why this trial was garnering so much attention.

When they got to the courtroom, it was packed. They wouldn't have had a seat if not for Sy's law clerk, who sat in the row behind Sy and Bryan telling people that the row was reserved for the family of the victim. Soon after Sara and Dorothy were seated, the court was called to order.

Emmons and Lockard were all smiles as the trial resumed.

Judge Maxfield motioned to the defense table. "Call your witness."

Emmons announced, "We call Dr. Carolyn Mann."

Dr. Mann had barely finished taking her oath when Emmons began the questioning.

Dr. Mann, what is your specialty?"

"I'm a psychiatrist. I work extensively with patients with debilitating diseases, such as those with cancer and AIDS."

"Was Hope Grossman your patient?"

"Yes. I was treating her for depression following her mastectomy."

"Did you consider her to be suicidal?"

"She told me she'd thought of suicide before but never intended to act on it. I got her to agree to a 'no harm' contract, which means that if she ever considered suicide, she'd call me so we could talk about it."

"Dr. Mann, did she ever call?"

"Yes. One morning she was particularly despondent. We talked, and then I phoned her husband and he spent the day with her. The crisis passed, and she seemed better at her appointment the next day."

"What are the symptoms for determining whether a patient is suicidal?"

"If they verbalize it, there's reason to be concerned."

"Are there other symptoms that aren't as recognizable?"

"Yes. Once a person decides to end his or her life, the person's behavior can be very misleading. The person can seem relaxed, almost happy, because he or she has it planned. The family may think the crisis is over."

"Thank you, Doctor."

Emmons turned to the prosecution table, smiling. "Your witness."

Sy Marcus approached the doctor in a friendly manner as he walked toward the jury. Then, turning and moving closer to the defense table, he asked his question in a loud, distinct manner. "Doctor, from your experience, have you determined whether depressed people are more likely to be poisoned by someone than non-depressed people?"

A wave of laughter rolled through the courtroom. Dr. Mann tried not to laugh as she answered, "No." Sy was pleased by the jurors' obvious signs of amusement. He had also succeeded in relaxing the witness.

"It wouldn't make any difference whether you were depressed or not if somebody stuck something in your drink and poisoned you, would it?"

"That's true."

"Even depressed people eat and drink, right?"

"Yes, they do."

Sy's demeanor hardened.

"Did you approve of her plans to vacation in the Bahamas?"

"Yes. I thought a vacation with her husband would be beneficial."

"Did you know Alfred Birmingham, the man she believed to be her husband's homosexual lover, would be on the yacht with her the first week?"

"No. Had I known, I would never have recommended the trip."

"Why is that?"

"In her mind, Alfie and Sammy's relationship caused her considerable anguish."

Syrus slid the suicide note exhibit in front of the doctor.

"Dr. Mann, it's already been established that Hope Grossman had consulted a divorce lawyer on at least one occasion. Isn't it possible she was referring to ending her marriage in this note, rather than suicide?" Reading from the note, Sy spoke reverently. "'I can't go on like this anymore. We have many happy memories, but I don't see any future for us.'"

"It's possible."

"No more questions."

After several character witnesses attested to Sammy and Alfred being solid citizens who had contributed to society and had no criminal history, the day appeared to end on a positive outcome for Sammy and Alfred.

Sy was heading toward the doors when a man stepped forward and pulled on his arm. "Excuse me, Mr. Marcus. You don't know me, but I'm Wendell Williams; Hope saved me from drowning in the Mississippi. I was trying to commit suicide. After what she said to me that day, I don't believe she would ever commit suicide. Is there anything I can do to help?"

Sy contemplated for a moment. "Thanks; we appreciate you coming forward, but I don't know if I can get you on the witness list at this time." Sy handed him his business card. "Call my office immediately and leave your name and number. I'll talk to the DA about it."

"Sure thing," Wendell said.

Sy shook his hand and handed him his card as he said, "Thanks for your support, and see if there is anyone you can tell your story to in the media; that would be a great help to us."

Wendell said, "Yes, I'll try."

As Syrus and Ramsey entered the hallway, a barrage of media people accosted them. Ramsey yelled, "We have no comment!" They turned the corner and went into an office where they could make their escape out a door to the back alley.

When Sy arrived home that evening, Rachel was waiting. Before he could say anything, she announced, "I want to go back to the courtroom so I can hear the rest of the trial. You don't need to recall me now, do you?"

"Sammy is being called to the stand tomorrow, and he's their last witness, so unless Ramsey wants to save you as a rebuttal witness to Sammy's testimony, I think it would be fine. I'll give him a call and let you know."

The next morning, it was windy and raining hard, which made it easier for Sy and Rachel, with an umbrella and raincoats on, to go unnoticed as they ducked into the courthouse through the back alley. They went into a private office to meet with Ramsey and the rest of the staff to discuss their strategy.

Sammy and Alfie had also come early so they could miss the media frenzy. They were in their holding room—a barren space with no windows or pictures, but only a small table with uncomfortable steel chairs with steel slat backs, reminiscent of a prison cell. They sat at the table drinking the coffee they had brought with them. Alfie had his arms crossed tightly against his chest and kept crossing and uncrossing his legs. Sammy remained cool. Alfie leaned into Sammy and said quietly, "I can't stand this, Sammy. What if we don't get off? I need a Xanax. Oh God, I can't go to prison; you know what they would do to me!"

Sammy pulled back, bristling. He got out of his chair and walked around the room. "Calm down, Alfie; you know I won't let anything happen to you."

"But what if that jury believed Rachel? Alfie raised his voice and emphasized every word. "She was believable."

"You're overreacting. There is no way the jury will find us guilty after I testify. Trust me!"

Just then a guard opened the door and stuck his head inside. "They're ready to start."

As they entered the courtroom, Sammy saw that Diane was back in the courtroom and sitting right behind him. He turned to her and leaned over the balustrade to give her a kiss on the cheek before taking his seat.

The court was called to order, and as the judge looked out over the crowded courtroom, he announced, "Call your witness."

Emmons stood. "We call Samuel Grossman to the stand."

Sammy slowly rose, turned to Diane, and briefly took his daughter's hand. Diane murmured, "I love you, Daddy." Sammy smiled at her while fighting back tears as he took his place on the witness stand.

Emmons began his questioning. "State your name for the record, please."

"Samuel Grossman."

"You were the husband of Hope Grossman at the time of her death?"

"Yes."

"And you have just one daughter?"

"Yes, our beloved Diane, and one beautiful grandson. They're all I have left."

"Sammy, did you murder Hope?"

"God, no! I loved her more than life itself. I would gladly take her place."

Emmons grabbed the indictment, his voice rising to a crescendo as he asked, "Did you conspire with Alfred Birmingham to willfully, deliberately, and with premeditation murder your wife Hope by poisoning, as this indictment written by Bryan Ramsey says?"

"*No* ... absolutely not!"

"There's something I would like to clear up. Have you ever taken an HIV test?"

"Yes, at my wife's request, and it was negative."

"Sammy, tell us about your relationship with your wife of over twenty-five years."

"We loved each other. We always saw each other through the worst of times. She was my best friend."

"Were you sexually compatible and happy?"

"Very compatible. I was totally satisfied with our sex life, as I believe she was as well."

"Are you now or have you ever been sexually attracted to men?"

"No, absolutely not."

"Then you are not homosexual, as has been charged?"

"No, I am not."

"Do you know if Alfred is homosexual?"

"Yes, he is."

"It's been observed that you spend a lot of time with Mr. Birmingham. So what kind of relationship do you have with Alfred?"

"He's my business partner and the older brother I never had. I also consider him to be my best friend."

"And why did you move in with Mr. Birmingham after your wife's death?"

"I'd been married my entire adult life … I had never lived alone. I couldn't bear the emptiness of that house." He stopped and looked over at the jurors. "Everywhere I looked, I saw Hope … heard her voice. I thought I was losing my mind, so I put the house up for sale and moved into Alfred's carriage house. He paused and then said, "On a temporary basis."

"Why not stay with your daughter?"

Emmons gestured toward Diane, who smiled reassuringly.

"Diane was very supportive, but their house was small and they were expecting a baby. Alfred had plenty of room, and his guesthouse was bigger than Diane's whole house, so it only made sense. He still had his privacy, and I had mine. He insisted I stay in the guesthouse until

I was more financially stable because we needed to pay down the debt we had accrued with our real estate ventures."

"When did you move out of your home with Hope?"

"After I put my house up for sale, I had one of the brownstones custom finished for me. In September, when we returned from our last business trip, it was completed and ready to move into, which I did."

In the background, Ramsey and Marcus were quietly making notes and whispering to each other.

"You mentioned a trip. Why have you and Mr. Birmingham traveled together so often?"

"We're importers. Our trips are business related, and Hope came along at least half the time. She was always welcome to join me."

"When Hope didn't go with you, did you call home regularly?"

"Yes, I made frequent calls to my wife and daughter. They always knew where I was and how to reach me. My daughter can confirm that if you'd like to ask her."

"No, that's not necessary. Tell us how your wife felt about your relationship with Alfred."

"Alfie and Hope were close friends." Sammy paused and then turned to the jury and with emphasis said, "Until Rachel tried to convince her we were lovers."

"Were Hope and Alfred still close at the time of her death?"

"Yes. He helped me plan her birthday party and was as concerned about her welfare as I was. That is why he wanted her to join him the first week of the vacation. We had to board the yacht because we had reserved it. Otherwise, we would have lost the use of it for weeks. I couldn't leave, so Alfred went and had Hope join him so she could get some much-needed rest before I arrived." Sammy began to tear up. "If only I had been there, maybe she would still be alive." Sammy covered his face to hide his tears.

"Yes, Sam, why didn't you go the first week?"

"When Mr. Morgan offered me the use of the corporate yacht, he offered it for two weeks. I didn't think about it; I just said yes. Then, when it was closer to the time to go, I could only close the warehouse and office for one week. I paid vacation pay to my employees for the

week, but I couldn't close the business for two weeks. No one can handle the business but me, so I asked Alfie, Hope, and Hope's dear friend Sharon to go on ahead. They only left five days ahead of when I was to join them for the next eight days."

Emmons softened his tone as he asked his next question. "I know this is very painful for you, but we must talk about Hope's emotional state in the last months of her life."

Sammy wiped his eyes, trying hard to maintain his composure. "She'd had a lot of disappointments, but the final blow was finding out she had breast cancer."

"If Hope committed suicide, why was there no evidence on the yacht?"

Sammy, barely able to answer, cleared his throat and tried to get himself together as he choked out his response. "Alfred said he found the letter in her cabin and hid it, thinking he was protecting me and Hope."

Syrus shot to his feet. "Objection, Your Honor; that's hearsay. If Mr. Birmingham wishes to take the stand, we would be happy to hear his testimony."

"Sustained."

"Let me rephrase the question. When, and under what circumstances, did you find out your wife took her own life?"

"I met Alfred at the airport. He flew home and arrived close to the same time as the arrival of the casket. When we were in the limo following the hearse …" Sammy began to cry again, and Emmons patiently waited for him to pull himself together. "He gave me the letter, and I couldn't believe what it said."

"How did that make you feel?"

"I felt like I had failed her. I was overwhelmed with grief. I still am."

The jury was enlivened while listening to Sammy; some of them wiped away tears, and some nodded knowingly. Alfie leaned forward to see the jury's reaction. His fascination at what he was witnessing was evident in his wry grin and gleeful eyes.

"Why did you decide to maintain and perpetuate the falsehood about her accidental death?"

"At that point, it would have only made it harder on everyone if I had told them she committed suicide. Moreover, she would have been buried in the potter's field with the criminals. She was the best woman I have ever known or will ever know, and she should be buried with the saints, certainly not the sinners. There is nothing I wouldn't have done to preserve the sanctity of her memory."

"Did you hide her suicide so you could collect the life insurance?"

"No! I wasn't even aware of the double indemnity clause until you brought it to my attention."

"And what did you do when you found out?"

"I immediately made arrangements to pay the money back, plus interest."

"No more questions, Your Honor."

Judge Maxfield said, "We'll take a fifteen-minutes break before we continue."

Marcus and Ramsey conferred during the break about how to handle the cross-examination of Sammy. Syrus said, "He's getting a lot of sympathy from the jury. We need to break the spell somehow."

"I expected this, but he's more believable than I had anticipated. I have some questions that I hope will rattle him. Was there anything you heard that might unravel his lies?"

"The fact that he has done nothing to honor Hope but he has spent money on a Rolex watch, a new car, and furnishing a new townhome."

As soon as the court reconvened, Ramsey began his cross-examination.

"You've never had a sexual relationship with Alfred Birmingham, the man you lived with for the past year?"

"Absolutely not. I said I lived in the carriage house, not in his house."

"You do, however, acknowledge the fact that Alfred is homosexual."

"Yes, I do."

"So you weren't concerned with how this might look to others?"

"No."

Ramsey got right in Sammy's face as he asked, "Then why were you so adamant with Rachel that she not discuss your little nude soiree with Alfred?"

"Because it didn't happen the way Hope said. I was afraid Rachel would twist it, as you have, just because Alfred is gay."

Ramsey looked at the jury as he asked the next question. "You seem awfully concerned about Alfred. Could there be something more here than the pure friendship you profess to have?"

"Just because Alfred is gay doesn't mean he can't be my friend or my business partner. A true friend doesn't judge his friend's sexuality. I know many straight men whose friends blatantly cheat on their wives. They may not approve, or do it themselves, but few end friendships over it!"

A few of Alfred and Sammy's supporters in the audience cheered. The judge rapped his gavel.

"Thank you for that stirring speech, Mr. Grossman. Can you tell us what your relationship with Sharon Chambliss is?"

He hung his head and lowered his voice. "She's just a good friend—a companion. I'm still in love with Hope." He straightened up and spoke clearly as he directed his speech to the jury. "There isn't a day that goes by I don't think about her and miss her terribly. It wouldn't be fair to ask another woman to compete with her memory."

Sammy, tearing up, looked to his daughter, who smiled back at him.

"You told this court earlier that you have made arrangements to pay back the million-dollar double indemnity insurance fraud; is that correct?"

"Yes."

Ramsey began his rapid-fire assault.

"But you had the use of the money for nearly a year. Did you make any charitable contributions in Hope's memory?"

"No."

"Did you put the money in the bank because you didn't need it?"

"Well, no, but—"

Ramsey stopped and roared, "No indeed! You called the insurance company the day after your wife's death because you desperately needed that money to save you and Alfred from bankruptcy. Isn't that true?"

"We were having a small cash flow problem—"

"Small problem? According to your banker, Mr. Gillpatrick, you were days away from going under when you were saved by that two-million-dollar payoff. Isn't that true?"

Sammy cocked his head and angrily said, "I was talking to several other banks and some real estate brokers who were interested in assuming the loan."

"What a nice coincidence your wife should accidentally die just when you needed that financial shot in the arm."

Emmons jumped up and shouted, "Objection! Improper question."

Ramsey grinned as he said, "I'll withdraw the question. Mr. Grossman, haven't you and Mr. Birmingham taken numerous expensive trips together?"

"As I said, we're importers. Our travel is business related, and we have the tax documentation to prove it."

"Yes, I'm sure you do. Anyone slick enough to get away with murder can certainly fool the IRS and an insurance company."

Emmons angrily bellowed, "Objection, Your Honor!"

"Sustained."

"After five years of being virtually inseparable, didn't you and Alfie decide it would be easier to be together, as well as becoming millionaires, if Hope were out of the way?"

Emmons jumped in again. "Objection, Your Honor. Badgering the witness."

"I withdraw the question. Mr. Grossman, you have already admitted you lied to your family and friends and to the insurance company. Isn't that true?"

"Well, yes, but I ..."

"Then how do we know what else you've lied about?"

"Objection, Your Honor!"

Ramsey backed away from the witness stand. "Withdrawn. You admit that you have not given one dime to honor the memory of your wife, Hope, correct?"

"There's been so much I had to do to save the investment property and to keep my import company running; I simply have not had the time."

"But you've had the time to take a trip to Europe for a month, furnish a townhome, and buy a new car and a Rolex watch, did you not?"

"Objection, move to strike. Not a proper question."

"I'll withdraw the question. I have a picture that has been entered into evidence—a picture of you and Alfred when you were in military school together. Would you please read what Alfred wrote on the back?"

Sammy's lip curled up as though in disgust as he read, "'To my best buddy, you are the only thing that makes this school bearable. My love is endless, Alfred.'"

Ramsey handed the picture to the judge. "You say you have never had a sexual relationship with Alfred, but this picture says, 'To my best *butty*,' as in 'buttocks' Are you going to lie to us about this picture?"

"We were fourteen and sixteen, and we were playing around. It wasn't serious. All the guys said they loved each other. It was a standing joke in the school. Anything to survive the harsh treatment we received."

"I do have one final question. Are you bisexual?"

Sammy looked at Alfie, took a breath, and stammered, "N-no."

Ramsey nodded at the jury. "No more questions."

Emmons stood. "The defense rests, Your Honor."

"It's getting late. We'll hear closing arguments on Monday morning."

Sammy leaned in to Emmons. "I need to speak with you alone. Can we meet later tonight?"

"Yes. I have to get back to my office now. You want to meet me at the River Front Club in an hour?"

"Sure, I'll see you there."

Ramsey and Marcus loaded their briefcases, and Marty scrambled to help them. Marcus bent over. A feeling of dread knotted in his throat as he said, "Bryan, we need to get together this weekend and try to salvage the trial. It appeared to me the jury believed his lies and was moved by his theatrics."

Bryan nodded and frowned, not looking at Syrus.

Marty, trying to bolster their morale, said, "I think you canceled out his pitiful theatrics and showed Sammy for the liar that he is."

Sy sighed. "We all know he did it, but the burden of proof is tough—in this case, much tougher than creating reasonable doubt."

Ramsey chimed in. "Yeah, it's going to take more than a brilliant closing argument to win this one. I hope you have a rabbit up your sleeve, Marcus!"

"Yeah, I'm going to have to go rabbit hunting. Give me the night to think. Let's get together tomorrow morning at my office, Bryan."

Bryan nodded.

As Sy entered the parking garage, he could see a woman standing by his car. With all the negative press this case had garnered, he was wary of strangers. As he got closer, he recognized Sharon, Sammy and Hope's supposed friend. She started walking toward him, looking around to see who else might see them. In a hushed voice, she said, "I need to talk to you; it's important."

Syrus smiled. He could see from her stricken look that she had something to say that he wanted to hear. "Let's get into my car."

She followed him, got in the passenger side, and started talking. "Syrus, I committed perjury on the stand. If I give you some valuable information, can you keep me from being prosecuted?"

Sy tried to keep from smiling. "Probably, but I can't guarantee anything. What is the valuable information?"

"I've been sleeping with Sammy and had been for months, including before Hope's death. I also know that he has had sex with Alfie, because he tells me that Alfie gives better head than I do."

Sy tried to muffle a gasp and keep a straight face. "Do you have any love notes or pictures of him and Alfie hugging, holding hands, or embracing?"

"No, Sammy has never liked taking pictures. He always told me he didn't want anything Hope could use in a divorce court, and I'm sure he told Alfie the same thing."

"Did you ever go to Alfie's house after Sammy moved in and see anything at all, like Sammy's clothes in the closet or his personal items in the master bathroom?"

"I was only there once to drop off a package, and I barely got in the front hall. He always came over to my house; he never had me over to the guesthouse he lived in."

"What was in the package?"

Sharon turned away and murmured, "Sex toys."

Sy was flabbergasted but maintained his composure as he thought, *Wow, Sammy really is a perverted Dr. Jekyll / Mr. Hyde.* "Did he say what the sex toys were for?"

"He said they were a gift for Alfie and his friends."

"Do you know any of Alfie's friends?"

"No."

"Do you know where he got the cyanide?"

"No."

"You were on the yacht when Hope died; did anything seem strange to you at the time?"

"Not really. I did think Alfie was acting a little too distraught, as if she were his lover."

"Do you know if Sammy or Alfie took a trip to the island before the incident occurred?"

"No, I just moved back to Memphis last year. I didn't start seeing Sammy until three months before Hope's death."

"You haven't given me anything I can use except that you lied. If we used you as a rebuttal witness now, it would be she said / he said and would probably backfire on us because Sammy is such a good liar and actor."

"Yes, when he was on the stand he was so convincing I had to stop and remember what I had heard from him. But he showed his true self last night when he threatened to kill me."

"You didn't by any chance get that on a recording?"

She bowed her head, tears trickling down her cheeks, "No. I wasn't thinking like that when I went to see him. I had no idea he could be so vindictive."

"We have closing arguments on Monday. I'll talk to Bryan and see what he thinks. In the meantime, if you think of anything or find anything we could use, preferably hard evidence that could possibly help us, give me a call."

She opened the door to get out. "Okay, I'll see what I can come up with."

Sy headed back to his office. As soon as he arrived, he went straight to the kitchen to get a cup of coffee. He was strung out from the emotional impact of dealing with the trial; it was much harder than he had anticipated. He couldn't keep the feeling at bay of the looming disaster if he lost the case. Everyone in the firm was busy ignoring him. He felt sure they knew he was losing the case and did not want to have to weigh in on the outcome. He closed his office door and started working on other cases. It always helped him to focus on cases he could win rather than the one that was making him doubt himself. Soon after, his secretary buzzed him to say she was leaving and asked if he needed anything before she left.

"You don't have a case of Stoli on you, do you?" he joked.

She laughed and told him to go home and get some rest. Unfortunately, home was the last place he could rest. Everyone was leaving the office for the night, which made it conducive for him to be able to focus on what he could do to win this trial. He was contemplating the fallout after the trial's end if Sammy got off. He was sure Diane would despise him and doubted she would have anything to do with Rachel again, which would hurt her deeply. He sighed as his foot beat a short, rhythmic thumping. He knew Sammy had done it. Years of working with criminals had honed his instincts.

As he was going over all the details of the trial in his head, something about the insurance payoff bothered him. The fact that the insurance company didn't try to find the coroner after they learned of Hope's death was not an accident. The company must have been informed that it was a suicide when they found out it was not an accidental death. Suddenly it struck him. Insurance companies do not pay in cases of suicide unless it has been two years after the purchase of the insurance policy; it was then that the epiphany pierced through the scrambled theories in his mind. Hope had been murdered two years and two months after Sammy bought the insurance policy. Sammy must have been planning her murder for that long. And probably he had only paid back one million dollars, so he was able to keep the other million dollars.

Suddenly all the pieces fell into place. At first, he was sickened by the thought but then a white-hot fury replaced it. It was all planned so meticulously. Sammy must have been patting himself on his back until his arm nearly fell off. Sy was not going to let Sammy get away with killing Hope. A brilliant closing statement was not going to win this case for them. There had to be something else: a rebuttal witness, someone who could testify to Sammy and Alfred being lovers—anything he could come up with that would throw a wrench into the case—a showstopper. He had the weekend to come up with something.

He called both of the detectives who had been working on the case with him and told them to find someone who would verify that Sammy and Alfred were lovers. There had to be someone who knew. He was so tired; he needed to rest for a minute and collect his thoughts. He leaned back in his chair, put his feet up on the desk, and closed his eyes to relax for a while.

A woman in a shimmering ball gown walked toward him. Her face was a blur, but when she called him by his Hebrew name, Shea Shalom, he immediately recognized Hope's voice. "I miss you all so much. I'm so alone here. It wasn't my time to die. Please help me, please, Shea Shalom."

Syrus startled, woke up, and quickly dropped his feet off the desk. Tears were streaming down his face as he rubbed his eyes, thinking, *Now I'm losing my mind.* He knew it was a dream, but such a vivid dream, unlike any dream he'd ever had before. At the end of the dream, Hope's face came into focus, as well as her mannerisms, and she was wearing the dress she'd had on at her celebratory birthday party. She was obviously distraught and crying out to him for help. He didn't know what to do or what to think. He did not want to tell Rachel; he knew what she would say. Trembling, he put his head in his hands, reflecting on what had happened. *"What could I do to help Hope? There must be something I'm supposed to know. Okay, God, if you are out there, this would be a good time to help me out.* Sy hung his head and pleaded for insight.

45

Sammy Grossman and Wayne Emmons were sitting at a table in the River Front Club bar. Sammy made the grand gesture of buying their drinks before starting to talk. "So how do you think I did?"

"A damn fine job, Sammy. The jury is leaning your way."

"So what do you think our odds of winning are?"

"We've certainly created a reasonable doubt. I'd say they're stacked in our favor."

Sammy shook his head. "Not good enough."

"What do you mean?"

Sammy looked around the restaurant bar, put his drink on the table, leaned in, and lowered his voice to a whisper as he stared straight into Emmons's face. "Hope didn't commit suicide. Alfie killed her; I've been protecting him."

Dumbstruck, Emmons nearly dropped his drink; his face turned red as he tried to control his anger. He clenched his teeth as he lowered his voice to a growl. "What the hell are you talking about? What about the suicide note?"

"She wrote that a few weeks before she died. She wrote me about a dozen of them when she was planning to divorce me."

"Why would Alfie kill her?" Emmons leaned in closer and asked in a whisper, "Are you two really ... lovers?"

"I've never had a sexual relationship with Alfie, or ever given him any indication that I wanted one. But he became obsessed with the idea over the years."

"That's why he killed her?"

"He's one sick little fuck. He joked about getting rid of her so we could be together. I had no idea he was serious about it."

"Why didn't you turn him in then?"

"I confronted him about it, and he threatened to say I'd planned it for the insurance money. I knew I couldn't bring back Hope. Our business dealings were so intertwined I was afraid they would believe him." Sammy leaned back. "Frankly, I never thought anyone would find out."

"Why on earth are you telling me this cock-and-bull story now?"

Sammy took a swig of his drink. "I've been watching Alfie during the trial, and I think he's about to crack. I want you to try to make a deal for me. I'm not going down with him."

"You can't make a deal now, Sammy! The defense has already rested. The state hasn't proven their case. The worst you'll get is a hung jury. I thought he was like your brother."

Sammy nonchalantly swirled his drink around the glass. "So how can I protect myself?"

Emmons grabbed him by the arm, squeezing it with all his strength. "If you bring this out now, Alfie will make accusations back, and you two will look like you've had a lovers' quarrel. If you open this can of worms, you'll virtually guarantee your conviction. My advice is to keep it to yourself!" Emmons let go of his arm, stood, and stormed toward the door without looking back.

46

Sy pulled into the driveway of his home, dreading having to face Rachel and her inquisition. When he walked in the back door, he was surprised to see Darlene Evans seated at the kitchen table. He stopped and politely said hello to Darlene, and then turned to Rachel, asking sternly, "Rachel, may I have a word with you in my office?"

She followed him to his office, and as soon as he shut the door, he started. "What is Darlene doing here?"

"She called me; Hope has made contact with her. Hope said she has been in court with you every day since Sammy was on the witness stand."

"Yeah, I knew someone was breathing down my neck."

"Hope wants to talk to you."

"Rachel, what's going on? What are you trying to do?"

"I'm not doing anything," Rachel said. She looked so earnest he could hardly be angry with her. "Hope wants to talk to you. Can't you at least listen to what she wants to tell you? What could it hurt?"

Sy leaned back in his chair. "If anyone were to hear about this, it would cost us this case and Sammy could go free. Are you are willing to pay that price?"

"After Sammy's testimony, I think we've already lost. No one will ever know; I swear. What have we got to lose?"

Sy was at his wit's end. He closed his eyes and rubbed his forehead as he considered a solution. The puzzle of the dream began to make sense, but he still had trouble believing he could talk with Hope. The only way to know would be to play along, if for no other reason than to solve the garbled riddle in his mind. He solemnly turned to Rachel, who was waiting patiently for his decision. "At this point, we don't have much to lose. Our case is weak, and there's plenty of reasonable doubt. It looks like Sammy is going to win. If we do this, it cannot be recorded, and it can never be discussed with anyone—ever. Make sure she understands that."

"I'll tell her."

Rachel left the room as Sy made his way to the window. He clenched his jaw as he stared into the night sky, wondering what could possibly be revealed about the murder that he didn't already know. Rachel, all smiles, reappeared with Darlene in tow. Rachel took charge, rearranging the chairs so the three of them could sit together. Rachel seated Darlene in front of Sy, dimming the lights as Darlene began to talk.

"Mr. Marcus, I want you to understand why I'm doing this. Most souls make the transition to the other side easily. Others, like Hope, have unfinished business. We refer to them as earthbound souls. They are not at peace and can't move on. Hope is living a hellish existence, and she needs our help to be able to let go of her anguish and anger. She has to be at peace before she can accept going to the light."

Sy smiled politely. "Ms. Evans, I believe your heart's in the right place, but you need to promise me this will never be discussed outside these four walls."

"I will preserve your confidentiality, Mr. Marcus, as God is my witness; I swear. Now, please … just try to relax. I need complete quiet while I meditate to call forth the spirit of Hope."

Moments passed. Sy began rubbing his hands together to calm his jittering nerves. When Darlene took a deep breath and started to talk, he could not believe it; he heard a semblance of Hope's voice. Sy stared prisons funded by the federal government. Prisons are becoming a for-profit business justified under the federal government's war on drugs.

"They don't care whose lives they ruin as long as they make money from it. It's all about power and greed. Congress now wants to take money from the federal housing budget to pay for federal prisons. They are intentionally disenfranchising poor people, as if they don't suffer enough. Then the federal government will blame the poor American cities like Memphis and say it's the city's problem—as if poor cities would have tons of money to spend. What part of 'poor' do they not understand?"

Rachel could see the rising anger in his demeanor. "I wish you would have talked to me about how you felt."

Sy grimaced. "The men in our family don't talk about feeling. I'm sure you've heard my dad say, 'Never forget where you came from; you're a Jew. You have to prove your worth every day with no complaints.'"

Rachel sighed. "Yes, I've heard him say that, but I always attributed it to being from Europe and surviving the pogroms. I hadn't considered the impact it had on you as a child."

Sy took a deep breath and sat up straight. "I always looked up to my dad. He came to America with nothing but the shirt on his back. He could speak four languages but didn't know English. He learned English very quickly and carved out a life for himself and us, with very little help from anyone. But he never forgave himself for not getting his parents here before the war. He and Uncle Morris tried, but his parents wanted them to get their siblings here first. His parents never got the chance to come; the Nazis had already murdered them. And Dad suffered because of it until the day he died."

Rachel nodded. "I know. We should not be complaining about anything, knowing what our parents and grandparents went through. We should be on our knees every day, thanking God for the life we have in America. And Sy, I do take responsibility for my mistakes—for not speaking up when I should have. I was so afraid it would escalate into a fight. We agreed on everything in the beginning. When we started having issues, I didn't want to rock the boat, so I kept quiet and stuffed my feelings. When I had stuffed enough of them, I lost control and blew up, which never helps to resolve the issue. My anger, mostly at myself, got the best of me. I really just want to have more time with you—a time when we can talk and work through our issues. Somewhere along the way, we stopped talking."

Sy nodded. "I take full responsibility for my part too. I promise that after this trial is over, we are going on a two-to-three-week vacation. And you know, I am serious about running for judge next year. It's the one place that maybe I could make a difference."

They continued to talk into the night, until Rachel was so tired, she took Sy's hand and said, "Darling, I've missed you so much. Please come to bed. I'll move all your things back into our bedroom tomorrow." Sy smiled, happy to return to their bed and even happier to be holding his wife in his arms again.

Sy put his hands on his thighs and began rubbing them back and forth, shaking his head. "It's not possible. There is no precedent, and I would be the laughingstock of the legal profession."

Rachel huffed, "So why can't you make it a precedent? What would it take to get the judge to allow the psychic on the stand?"

Sy said, "I'll have to think about that. I've exhausted all legal possibilities, and the thought of losing the trial and Sammy winning is unacceptable. Anything would be better than losing. I'm so tired; I'm going to bed. I have to sleep on it."

Rachel woke up early the next morning. Groggy, she turned to touch Sy, but he was not in bed or in the bathroom. She put on her robe and headed for the kitchen to make some coffee. She was surprised to see the lights on in Sy's study. She peeked in the door to see him in his robe, flipping through piles of books lying open on his desk. Sy looked up at her and said, "What are you doing up so early?"

"That was my question. Are you working on the closing argument?"

"No, I'm working on winning this case. I have a real farfetched idea."

"Really? What is it?"

"The only way we can get to the truth, because the truth is more important than winning. Even if we lose, everyone will know Sammy for what he is—a murderer!"

"What are you planning?"

"I'll tell you, and then I want you to decide if you think I should do it, because it'll affect both of us for a long time to come."

"Why?"

"Because fifty percent of my income is from criminal law, and it'll probably ruin my criminal practice. In fact, it could destroy my entire legal career, and losing that income is going to change things dramatically for us."

"I can live with that. It will be more of a sacrifice for you, and I appreciate what you're doing for Hope and me. I won't forget it."

"Yeah, well, my law partners aren't going to be so happy. They may even try to have me committed after this." Sy chuckled to himself.

Rachel insisted, "We have plenty of money, and we could sell this house. I'm in love with you; I've always loved you. We could live in an igloo for all I care."

Syrus moved to Rachel and pulled her close in an embrace. She welcomed his touch with tears in her eyes.

"I love you, Rachel. I don't want to lose you. You are my world; I'd be lost without you."

"Rachel smiled. "And you are all that matters to me."

Sy kissed her gently and pulled her in as close as possible as he whispered in her ear, "When this is over, let's get out of town—go to a deserted island."

"I've missed you so much." She ran her hands under his robe, where he had on nothing but his boxers. She moved her hands up and down his body, kissing his chest, slowly moving lower. He pulled her up to him and kissed her voraciously as he gently guided her into the guest bedroom across the hall. He swept her up and laid her on the bed. Suddenly he wanted her as powerfully as when he was with her the first time. His hands explored her every curve. As he gazed into her azure eyes, he could see the raw intensity of her desire for him as she abandoned herself to his magical touch. Her lips were filled with a hunger as their bodies melted together. There was nothing else in the world beyond their blissful orgasmic blending. Rachel felt what she could only describe as their spirits spinning together outside time and space, in a peacefulness that did not exist on earth.

They held each other for a long time. Both in a joyous embrace with Rachel's arms tight around Sy's back, holding him close as her tears of joy flowed freely.

Early that afternoon, they were back in Sy's study, working on the case together. Sy called Bryan and went over what he was about to do. He called Bryan several times explaining what he was planning. Rachel

Syrus stood up. "Your Honor, I'd like to call a rebuttal witness." One could have heard a pin drop as everyone waited to hear the name. "I call Darlene Evans, a noted medium, who will channel Hope Grossman's spirit so the victim can tell who the real killers are."

Gasps and whispers came from the audience as Emmons shot to his feet.

"That's ridiculous … It's outrageous!"

"Murdering Hope Grossman was outrageous," Sy countered.

The judge rapped his gavel, demanding silence from the audience.

Emmons, with his eyes glaring and face flushed red said, "May we approach the bench, Your Honor?"

Judge Maxfield motioned the attorneys forward.

All four of the attorneys assembled in front of the judge. Ramsey looked as though he wished he were invisible. Judge Maxfield, in a stern voice, said, "All right, gentlemen. Let's have it."

Emmons spoke first. "Your Honor, we have not been informed of this witness."

Syrus curtly replied, "Your Honor, we weren't informed of a suicide defense until their opening statement. We'd like to call Mrs. Evans, to prove it wasn't suicide. I have sworn affidavits from the police chief and an FBI agent to testify to her credibility." Sy handed the papers to the judge.

"What does the prosecution propose to do with this medium?"

"She'll channel the spirit of Hope Grossman and prove—"

Lockard cut in. "What are you trying to pull, Syrus? We're going to have a séance now, in court? Your Honor, this is crazy!"

The judge squirmed in his chair. "You are kidding, aren't you?"

Emmons started laughing, gesturing broadly. "Your Honor, we have a south-side witch we'd like to follow up with."

Syrus remained dead serious as he continued. "Judge, if you'll let me finish."

Emmons interjected, "Your Honor, there's no precedent!"

Syrus seized the subject as though cued. "I agree, Your Honor; there is no precedent … in the legal annals. But there is a precedent in this

Bible!" Sy grabbed the court Bible and thrust it toward heaven with the fervor of a revival evangelist.

"This Bible tells of mediums, spirits, and angels speaking to men throughout the Old and the New Testaments—this very book that every witness swears his oath upon because we believe it to be the word of God!"

Emmons scoffed, "That's ludicrous!"

Judge Maxfield's eyes narrowed as he lowered his glasses to stare through Emmons. "Excuse me, Mr. Emmons, are you saying the Bible is not valid?"

"No, of course not, Your Honor. However, using the Bible in this way is highly irregular. We are not prepared to argue this. We ask for a recess until tomorrow."

"Mr. Emmons, I don't think you need until tomorrow to dispute the Bible as the word of God. Mr. Marcus, if you're serious about this, I'll allow foundation to be made in front of the jury because I don't want to hear it twice. We'll reconvene in thirty minutes."

He rapped his gavel, and the guards moved in to escort Sammy and Alfie out as Emmons and Lockard rushed from the courtroom.

Emmons and Lockard walked stone-faced to their private chambers. As soon as they were in the room and closed the door, they broke out in laughter and hit each other on the back. Emmons proclaimed, "Thank you, Jesus! A psychic. I was afraid they'd come up with a gay witness … or pictures or something."

"Yeah, me too! But it looked like the jury was dying to see this. If we try to block it, it'll look like we have something to hide."

"Block it? Are you kidding? This is a God-blessed gift! Even if they don't turn the courtroom into a total circus, we can still get it reversed. We can't exactly consent to it, though. For the record, we've got to object … but just lay off on the argument. Judge Maxfield is just crazy enough to allow it, and we'll be guaranteed a new trial."

"You think she can really channel Hope Grossman?"

Emmons shook his head, smirking at Lockard's naivete. "I can't believe Sy would try this, or that he got Ramsey to go along with it. They must really be desperate."

Lockard huffed. "Or crazy. Who, in their right mind, believes you can talk to the dead or would admit to it in court?"

"Right, and then using the Bible as precedent? Leave it to Sy Marcus to come up with that to win over Judge Maxfield. Gotta give him credit, though, he's got—whatta they call it—chutzpah!"

"Yeah! So are you going to go talk to Sammy and Alfie, or do you want me to?"

Emmons considered the question. "I'll go. Sammy is the one to convince; Alfie will go along with anything he says." He picked up his file and headed for the holding room where Sammy and Alfie were waiting, smiling broadly as he entered the room.

"Well, boys, I believe the tide has turned in our favor! Marcus is going to put a psychic on the stand; he has really gone off the deep end. It's a hoax to begin with, and we believe it will turn off most people, especially the jury. Even if this psychic can fool the judge into believing she's Hope, I'll tear her apart on cross-examination and you'll get a not-guilty verdict. And if our Bible-thumping judge rules her testimony is admissible, we'll get a new trial. I can't offer you a better deal than that. It's a win-win situation."

Sammy nervously leaned in, looking at his intertwined hands, his thumbs going round and round as if they were chasing each other. With a scowl, he asked, "Are you sure nothing can go wrong?"

"Marcus is just grandstanding. There's no foundation for anything like this. It could only help our case at this point. You have nothing to worry about. I have to go prepare." Emmons turned and abruptly left the room.

Alfie slumped over in his chair with his arms crossed in resignation, staring at the floor. He glanced up at Sammy, who was cold and composed. Alfie, colorless, could barely breathe as he groaned, "I don't like this. I think mediums can channel the dead. What if Hope does come through her?"

"Oh, for Pete's sake, Alfie, that's ridiculous! They are just acting! If it bothers you, don't look at her. Just keep your head down and your mouth shut. Didn't you hear Wayne? This is a win-win situation. This guarantees we'll get out of this!"

"Then can we be together again?"

Sammy turned on him in disgust, "Even if we win, everyone will be watching every move we make. Then Marcus will probably sue us in a civil action. So no, we can't be together. I don't want anything or anyone to have information that could be used against us in court."

"I've ruined everything. I told you I couldn't do this. I'm not like you."

"Shut up! They could have this room tapped. And stop whining; you're worse than a woman."

49

THE COURT RECONVENED, AND THE ROOM WAS QUIET AS SYRUS BEGAN.

"This nation and its system of justice were founded upon biblical principles and a belief in the Almighty. That involves the doctrine of the immortality of the soul, the promise of eternal life." Syrus looked around the room and could see everyone listening intently. Even Judge Maxfield was nodding in agreement.

Sy picked up the Torah/Bible he had brought from home and gently kissed it. As he elevated the Bible, the sun streaming through the windows glistened on the gold letters, sparkling as he declared, "May the lord lead us to the truth today."

As he balanced the book in one hand, he opened it to a marked passage and declared, "Here, right here, in First Samuel 28:8, it tells about Saul going to the witches of Endor to contact the spirit of Samuel for advice before going into battle. Through a medium, Samuel's spirit told Saul that he and his sons would die the following day in battle ... and they did. Saul talked to Samuel's spirit."

Sy turned to see Rachel beaming as he thumbed through the Bible. "If you're more familiar with the New Testament, there are numerous references to Jesus speaking to the spirits of Moses and Elijah—men who'd been dead for hundreds of years. Most religions teach we have a mortal body and an immortal soul. Why can't a soul speak to a person if it so desires? And if that person believes and is open to it"—Syrus hit a fever pitch—"as Jesus said, all things are possible to he who believes!"

Syrus walked back to his table, laid the Bible down, and picked up a fat file folder.

"I have documentation that proves our next witness, Darlene Evans's, has the ability to communicate with the dead. All we are asking, Your Honor, is to let Hope Grossman's spirit have its day in court, just as you would do for any immortal soul, because we are *not* just mortals; we are all immortal souls. This is the only way we will ever get to the truth."

The room was silent as Syrus took his seat. Maxfield was beaming, moved by Sy's speech. "That was quite an argument, Mr. Marcus. Mr. Lockard? Mr. Emmons? Do you wish to comment?"

Emmons rose. "Your Honor, we feel this is too ridiculous to even argue, and we object strenuously to such antics. However, on the chance that you do consider allowing this witness, we'd like to pose a question. How can we be certain it's Mrs. Grossman's spirit speaking through this medium?"

"Your point is well taken."

Sy jumped to his feet. "Your Honor, we have anticipated this, and we believe we have a satisfactory solution."

"And what is that, Mr. Marcus?"

"Your Honor, we have a sworn deposition that Darlene Evans never met Hope Grossman or her mother. We suggest you interview Hope's mother, Sara, to determine a few questions that only Hope could answer. Once Mrs. Evans has called for the spirit, ask her the questions. When you're satisfied Mrs. Evans is channeling the spirit of Hope Grossman, allow me to question her concerning her death." Sara looked uneasy, but Rachel and Dorothy encouraged her to be strong. "Is this agreeable to the defense?"

Emmons proclaimed half-heartedly, "Of course not, Your Honor. We renew our objections to the entire procedure for the reasons already stated."

The judge grimaced. "So noted." He removed his glasses, rubbed his eyes, and then slowly put the glasses back on, clearing his throat.

"I've had to make some difficult rulings in my years on the bench, but none quite as unusual or difficult as this one." He stopped for a moment, leaving everyone in suspense, waiting for his answer. He laid his glasses on the desk, rubbed his eyes again, and then solemnly announced, "I have decided to allow the rebuttal witness to testify. However, I won't rule on Mrs. Evans's testimony until after I've heard the responses to the questions."

Gasping, followed by a noisy commotion, broke out in the courtroom. Sy was all smiles, but Ramsey, motionless, stared at the wall. Lockard and Emmons exchanged sly smiles. The judge pounded his gavel. "Order in the court! Order in the court! Bailiff, please escort Hope Grossman's mother to my chambers."

After the judge left the bench, some people left the courtroom for a short break.

Reporter Don Heller was headed back to the courtroom when he spotted Darlene Evans. He approached her. "My, Ms. Evans, what a stunning dress you're wearing. You don't look like how I would picture a psychic."

"Thank you; I guess that's a compliment."

"Yes, it is. I'm Don Heller with the *Memphis Daily News*. May I ask you a few questions?"

"Yes."

"Why are you doing this in court, of all places?"

"I'm trying to help this family and the soul that is trapped in the earth plane. She needs our help to be able to go into the light."

"That's noble of you. Is there any other reason you would be doing this?"

"Yes, hopefully to enlighten people—only those people who want to be enlightened, of course."

"I write for the newspaper. Do you have a message that I can quote?"

"Yes, you can quote this: Our natural state is that of eternal life. The body is a temporary vessel to house the soul. People need to understand you can never murder the soul."

"Is that it?"

Darlene smiled thoughtfully and beamed as she said, "We all need to love more and judge less."

Just as Mr. Heller started to ask another question, a bailiff came out to tell Darlene she would be called to the stand in just a few minutes. Heller thanked her and returned to the courtroom.

After the judge was seated, he announced, "Mr. Marcus, you may call your witness."

Syrus stood and looked to the back of the room. "The state calls Darlene Evans."

The double doors in the back of the courtroom swung open, and Darlene Evans walked down the aisle in a gorgeous holly-green dress with matching jacket designed by Rachel. The color, with her red curly locks flowing to her waist, accentuated her complexion, giving her a more youthful glow. She took the stand and was sworn in by the clerk. Syrus stepped up beside her and turned to face the jury.

"Ladies and gentlemen of the jury, members of the audience, you are about to witness something that has, to the best of my knowledge, never been done in a modern court of law. Darlene Evans will attempt to channel the spirit of Hope Grossman so we can find out the truth about her death. Regardless of your personal beliefs, we would appreciate complete silence and respect."

Sammy looked smugly skeptical while Alfred stared at the floor in desolation. Everyone was focused on Darlene. She dropped her head and seemed to go limp. The courtroom was as quiet as a tomb while everyone waited to see what transpired. Seconds passed like hours.

Sara struggled to see Darlene. Rachel was calm. However, nothing was happening, and even though Syrus appeared to be composed, a single drop of perspiration trickled down his temple.

Emmons glanced skeptically at Bryan Ramsey, who quickly looked away.

Diane frowned; arms crossed. Suddenly Darlene moved, grabbing everyone's attention, but then nothing happened.

Rachel was on the edge of her seat, as excited and scared of this daring feat as Syrus. Sara cringed as she covered her eyes, unable to watch any longer.

Judge Maxfield looked at Syrus, who gestured to be patient. A slight whisper rolled through the courtroom, and the judge raised his finger to his lips for silence.

Syrus straightened his tie, which was beginning to feel like a noose around his neck. He was startled when Darlene gasped deeply, straightened up, and opened her eyes. Her head was tilted to one side, and she looked at Sy but said nothing.

Sy anxiously stepped up. "Hope, this is Syrus."

Darlene/Hope slowly focused on Sy. "Syrus, I'm so alone." As she spoke, her voice, the cadence of her speech pattern, the way she cocked her head, and the way she gracefully whisked away hair from her face with her left hand, were all distinctly Hope's mannerisms.

Diane stared at the psychic, shocked at what she was seeing. *Did the psychic know my mother?*

"Syrus …"

Syrus quickly cut her off. "Hope, you're in a courtroom. You are on the witness stand. The judge is going to ask you some questions. Will you answer them truthfully?"

"Yes."

"When the judge is finished, I have some questions for you."

Darlene/Hope slowly shifted her focus to the judge, who gripped his note cards. Syrus stated, "Go ahead, Your Honor. You are talking to the spirit of Hope Grossman."

The judge cleared his throat. "Hope, can you tell me why you were sent home from school in the third grade?"

"Oh my, I was so embarrassed … it was recess … I had a little accident. They had to call my mother to take me home to change my clothes."

Sara gasped as she quickly covered her mouth. Rachel hugged her mother as she began to cry quietly. Diane leaned forward. Sammy's confident sneer was gone, replaced with shock. Alfie looked pale as his white-knuckled hands gripped his chair. He could not take his eyes off her.

Dorothy leaned over to Sara and Rachel, whispering, "That is your Hope; look at her hands and the way she moves." Rachel quickly shushed her.

"Hope, what was the secret you and your mother kept from your father when you were fifteen?"

"Mom found out I was seeing a gentile boy and made me give back his ring or she was going to tell Dad."

Sara gasped and slumped in her seat. Rachel asked Marty to help Dorothy get her mother out of the courtroom quietly.

The judge finished his questions. As he dropped his cards on the desk, he said, "This witness has correctly answered the questions provided in advance. Mrs. Evans has signed a sworn affidavit that she did not know Hope and has never spoken with Hope's mother prior to today. Mr. Marcus, you may proceed."

Syrus moved in. "Hope, it's Syrus. I want to ask you some questions, okay?"

"Yes."

"Hope, tell me what happened on the day you died."

Alfie was sweating and beginning to tremble. Sammy appeared to be looking for an exit.

Darlene/Hope began her story. "I was in the galley eating a bagel before I took my pills when Alfie came in. He asked me to pour him a cup of coffee. I poured Alfie a cup of coffee and then sat back down. I took my pills and then took another bite of my bagel. Soon after, I started to choke and felt sick, so I went into the bathroom that was nearby. I choked and choked and could not breathe. I tried to ask for help, but I couldn't speak. I passed out, and the next thing I knew, I was above my body, looking down. Alfie knocked on the door asking if I was okay; then he opened the door, checked my pulse, wiped my mouth, and just left me there and locked the bathroom door. I followed him as he went back to the table and picked up one of my bottles of pills. I followed him outside to the railing and watched him open the pill bottle and drop the pills into the ocean. Then he dropped the empty bottle into the water. He went back to the bathroom door and started screaming for help. After that, they dragged my body out and tried to revive me.

"The next thing I knew, my body was in a morgue and I could hear Alfie talking in the hallway, so I went out and listened. He said, 'Sammy, it's done. It was horrible, but it's done. I'm at the morgue; here's the number to call to stop the autopsy. Ask for Dr. Singh.' I didn't know why Sammy would want me to die, but I knew that was what he wanted because I could hear every word he said and every thought he had. He was happy he had gotten rid of me."

"Hope, Sammy is on trial for your murder. He's over there." Syrus pointed to Sammy, whose face was set in a defiant smirk.

Darlene/Hope turned slowly, and as she shifted her focus to see him, her voice filled with anguish as she cried out, "Why, Sammy? Why did you hurt me? *Why?* You said I was your best friend! Why did you want to hurt me?"

Alfie stared in shock at Darlene/Hope. He covered his face as he began to sob. Diane stood up and moved toward the aisle. "Momma! I'm here!"

Darlene/Hope turned to focus on her. "My angel, I miss you so much. I didn't want to leave you."

"Momma, I miss you too! You have a grandson."

Sammy jumped up, furious, as he screamed out, "She's a fake!"

He reached out for Diane, who was now at the railing. "Diane, believe me; that is not your mother."

Diane cast a look of disbelief and hatred at Sammy. Alfie cried out, "Oh my God! Please forgive me, Hope! I'm so sorry! It wasn't my idea, I swear!"

Sammy grabbed Alfie, shaking him. "Shut up, you idiot. This is a hoax!"

Sammy moved in front of the table, addressing the jury as Emmons tried to block him and make him shut up. Sammy pointed to Alfie. "He's a sick, demented liar. He killed her. I didn't do anything, and I can prove it!"

Pandemonium broke out in the courtroom, and the judge pounded his gavel. The judge signaled the bailiff to subdue Sammy, who was pulled away screaming, "I'm innocent! I tell you I'm innocent!"

Lockard rose. "I move for a mistrial, Your Honor!"

"Motion granted. Bailiff, take these defendants into custody." The judge rapped his gavel and abruptly left the bench, followed closely by Emmons, Lockard, and Ramsey. While two guards were forcibly removing Sammy from the courtroom. Another guard joined the bailiffs with Alfie in tow. The jury was filing out as Sammy continued to scream, "I didn't do anything. I'm innocent!"

Reporters rushed to the exit as guards directed the confused audience out of the courtroom.

As the courtroom emptied, Rachel made her way to Diane, who stood looking at Darlene/Hope with tears running down her face. Rachel took her niece in her arms as she broke down. She gently guided Diane to the witness stand, where Darlene/Hope, enveloped in a soft white light, smiled at her and touched first Diane's face and then Rachel's. Syrus joined Rachel and Diane. As Hope dropped her hand to her lap, Diane grabbed it and held on to it, crying, "Momma, Momma."

Hope spoke first to Rachel and Syrus, and then to Diane. "There are no words to explain what you've done for me. You have given me great peace—a peace that words cannot describe. I can see the light. I can feel the love." Hope/Darlene squeezed Diane's hand. "Diane, even though we might not be together, know that I am always here to love you. I will watch over you and your son. I'll always be here for you—always."

The glowing light began to fade, and Darlene's head dropped. Diane pulled on her hand as she wailed mournfully, "Momma, don't go."

Diane broke down sobbing. Rachel held her close as she cried with her. Darlene sat quietly for a moment, regaining her strength. Syrus helped her from the witness stand, smiling and telling her it had gone very well. Sy and Rachel hugged Darlene and then looked into each other's eyes with a renewed understanding. Rachel knew intuitively that the spiritual journey they had just gone through together was only the beginning as she put one arm around Syrus and the other around Diane. Syrus put one arm around Rachel and his other arm around Darlene as they huddled together. The four of them walked out together, crying and hugging each other.

Acknowledgement

To the many people who helped me with this manuscript. First and foremost (my husband of beloved memory) Sy Rosenberg and my dear friend, Stephanie Warren, both who believed in me when no one else did.

For two amazing editors, Jordan Rosenfeld and Debra Ginsberg, for their incredible insight and patience with all of my rewrites.

To all the others who contributed; Robertson G. Morrow, Dr. Harry Schaffer, Roger Lewis, D.D.S., Dan Tana and Mace Neufeld.

For their encouragement, time, and expertise I am eternally grateful.